Sweet Talk

Samantha Tonge

Printed in the United Kingdom

First Printing, 2013 Alfie Dog Limited

The author can be found at: authors@alfiedog.com

Cover images: © www.stevepopemedia.co.uk – with thanks to Sugar Mouse, a most wonderful sweet shop in Easingwold, North Yorkshire.

ISBN 978-1-909894-02-0

Published by
Alfie Dog Limited
Schilde Lodge, Tholthorpe,
North Yorkshire, YO61 1SN
Tel: 0207 193 33 90

DEDICATION

For my much-missed mum, Christine – a true
sweetheart.

CONTENTS

ACKNOWLEDGMENTS

Firstly, I'd like to thank Rosemary Kind for this opportunity, her enthusiasm and hard work. Also my short story writer friends, for their support – Tina K Burton, Alana Duffy, Pat Posner and Geraldine Ryan.

Thanks to Dad, Evelyn, Spen and Anna for their continued interest – same to the Tonge clan.

Plus a very special acknowledgement for Martin, Immy and Jay, who've always encouraged me to turn "I can't" into "I can".

1
SPICE UP YOUR LIFE

Nicky smiled at Gran, after enjoying a large mouthful of Battenburg cake.

'Thanks, Gran,' she said. 'I deserve this, after the day I've had. I thought GCSEs were difficult, until moving into the Sixth Form. Now the work is on a whole new level, altogether.' She took another bite of the pink and yellow sponge and closed her eyes as, effortlessly, it dissolved in her mouth - so much for the New Year resolution which was supposed to transform her into a dynamic, attractive fashion goddess.

Gran smiled. There was nothing more satisfying than someone appreciating her homemade cakes.

'I'm glad to see you've stopped your diet, love,' she said.

Nicky opened her eyes. 'Well, I think I've done well, cutting down on sweet stuff since January the First. Do you know, the average time that people stick to their New Year's resolutions? I've clocked up almost two months.'

Patricia smiled. Dear Nicky was always coming out with bits of trivia – recent ones being that butterflies taste with their back feet and that the plastic bits, on the end of shoelaces, are called aglets

'A fortnight?' said Patricia.

Nicky shook her head. 'Try halving that – it's only one week.'

Patricia chuckled. 'But was it my imagination, or did I spy you eating chocolate on Valentine's Day, a couple of weeks ago?'

Nicky's cheeks tinged pink. 'Blame Mum and Dad! I'd no date for the most romantic day of the year, so they took pity and bought me my favourite praline truffles. It would have been rude not to eat them.' She sighed. 'You're right, though. I've no willpower. Truth be told, I cheated throughout January.' She put down her coffee cup. 'If only I could lose half-a-stone, I'd look more like those catwalk models.'

Patricia gave a loud tut. 'And what would that achieve, dear? You're lovely and slim already.'

'It might boost my confidence,' she muttered. 'You should see Ashley Jones from my Art class – all long legs, and flat tummy. She got *four* Valentine's Day cards.' Nicky shook her head. 'My life seriously needs spicing up.'

'Agreed – visiting gran isn't the most glamorous activity for a teenage girl.'

'I didn't mean that! I love visiting you, it's just...'

Patricia's eyes twinkled, as she took off her gold-rimmed glasses. 'It's all right, love. I'm only teasing.' She stood up to turn off a dripping tap. 'If you really want to spice up your life, then you should stop obsessing about a few pounds in weight. How about... I don't know... resolving to follow your dreams, instead?'

Nicky shrugged. 'Well, I've already decided on a uni course. There's a degree up North where you get to do a paid placement, in a fashion house. But I'll really need to stand out in the interview – everyone wants an offer from them.'

'So how about resolving to spend the rest of the year

doing something that will help achieve that goal, instead of worrying about how much you weigh?'

Nicky's cheeks felt hot. 'Guess you think I'm silly...'

'Goodness no, – we all care about our appearance. Only yesterday, I bought a new pot of cream that promises to make me look a decade younger.'

Nicky giggled as Patricia shook her head.

'You're a sensible girl, love. I'm sure you know that losing that magic half-a-stone won't suddenly make your life perfect. Whereas doing all you can to get on that degree course could make a real difference.'

Nicky sipped her coffee. 'You know I tried getting that Saturday job, in *Beth's Boutique*, but the other applicants had experience - I didn't stand a chance.' She put down the coffee mug and unbuttoned her purple cardigan. Then she gazed at Patricia, trying to imagine her as a young woman 'What sort of stuff were you interested in, Gran, at my age?'

'I'm not sure... Life had got busy by the time I was seventeen.'

'Were you already working in the pencil factory?'

'Yes.'

Nicky pulled a face.

'Don't knock it, missy!' said Patricia and grinned. 'Without computers, pencils were big business back then! Over time we diversified into ranges of art pencils... It was tiring, boxing them all, but my colleagues were good fun.' She stared into the distance for a moment. 'I really missed them when I gave up work to have your auntie Jo. Anyway... at your age, I'd work on my feet, all day, and then head straight back home to help Mum with the cooking and housework. There were no ready-meals or dishwashers...'

'No online social networking, either,' said Nicky and grimaced, as if that were the worst thing in the world.

Patricia smiled. 'No, we made friends with people *in the flesh*, instead of via a computer screen! The highlight of the week was the Friday night youth club dance. Right from a young age, my dad would stand me on his feet and dance me around the living room, so I had some idea of what to do. Ah, what happy days...'

'Didn't you ever worry about your figure – although I'm sure you looked fab,' Nicky hastily added.

Patricia patted her granddaughter's hand. 'Times were different then, love. There wasn't so much pressure. Of course, we all wanted to look like the film stars, but we were more interested in their hair and clothes, than the size of their waistbands.' Patricia smiled. 'And my mother wouldn't have stood for any of that nonsense. I remember once, saying that my ankles were too fat. She said I clearly had too much time on my hands, if I was thinking about such things, and put me on gardening duty for a month! I thought it was most unfair.'

'Ooh, harsh!' Nicky grinned, as she tried to picture her gran as a sulky teenager.

'I thought Grace Kelly was the most stylish woman in the world and would have done anything to look like her.'

'Did you know that her middle name was Patricia?' said Nikky.

Her gran grinned 'Trust you to even know trivia about someone born well before your time! Yes, I was very proud of that! She was a real style icon, with her classy but fashionable dress sense. We covered up more, back in the Fifties, you see. I loved my knee-length poodle skirts for dancing at the youth club. No one wore such revealing clothes as you see girls in nowadays, so I don't suppose I was as conscious of my body as you modern young things...' Her eyes crinkled. 'Oh dear - do I sound my age, dear?'

'Never in a million years!' Nicky's eyes crinkled back. 'Although not all teenagers wear skimpy clothes now, you know...'

Patricia nodded. 'You've been blessed with a great sense of style. Stand up and let me have a gander at what you're wearing today.'

Nicky's chair scraped back and she twirled from side-to-side, so that her long, moss-green skirt flared out.

'And you made that yourself?' said Patricia. 'The green goes lovely with that purple cardigan. You have a natural talent for matching colours. And that's a really exotic looking belt.'

'I found it in the animal rescue charity shop, in town,' said Nicky, and fingered the bejewelled buckle. 'There's some real vintage stuff in there. I'm not even sure the shop assistants know how much a lot of it is worth.'

'That's it!' said Patricia, her eyes sparkling. 'Why don't you volunteer there? It'll give you the experience you need, in retail and you'll be able to put your fashion knowledge to good use, with all those donated clothes.'

'Gran! That's an awesome idea!'

'Why don't you give them a ring, right now? Their number will be in the phone book? Strike whilst the iron's hot, that's what I say...'

'Sounds like a plan!' said Nicky and got up to hug her gran...

Although when it came to it, the following Saturday, Nicky had reservations. Sure enough, the phone call had been successful – the shop's manager had said to come in for a chat and look around. But now her stomach twisted and she peered through the glass window as she stood in front of the charity shop. There were rails of clothes in the middle, with shelves of books, DVDs and ornaments across the side and back walls. Behind the cash desk, stood a lad, just a bit older than her. He was serving a man in a flat cap and raincoat. They were sharing a joke and before the customer left, they shook hands.

With a deep breath, Nicky collapsed her umbrella, shook it and then made her way in. After pushing her way around the rails of clothes, she arrived at the cash desk. At that moment, a slim lady in her forties, wearing a bright red blouse and grey trousers, appeared from a back room. A mackintosh was draped over her arm.

'Hello... I'm... I rang up yesterday about helping out,' said Nicky, to the woman, who immediately held out her hand.

'Nicky?' She beamed. 'I'm Jill – you spoke to me on the phone.' She turned to the young man, as she began to put on her coat. 'This is Ben. He'll help show you the ropes. Unfortunately I've got to pop into another of our shops this morning. They've had a plumbing problem over-night and some of the stock is ruined. Is that okay Ben?'

'It would be my pleasure.' He beamed. 'It's quiet, anyway. The bad weather always puts people off.'

Jill gave another broad smile. 'Okay, must dash – sorry I can't stay longer, Nicky, but I should be back in a couple of hours, to see how you're doing.'

With that she was gone and the two young people stood alone. Ben jerked his head towards the backroom door. 'There's a coat stand in there. Leave your bag and brolly in the cupboard by the sink. Then I'll fill you in on the essentials.' His chocolate eyes twinkled. 'I'd give you a personal tour of out back, but I don't like to leave the till.'

Stomach still twisting, Nicky headed out to the back room. Stacked high were boxes and bags, overflowing with toys and clothes and linen. She stashed her handbag in the cupboard by the sink and then went back out to Ben.

'So... Jill mentioned that you're interested in a career in fashion? This seems like an unlikely starting point,' he said and grinned. Despite her nerves, Nicky grinned back. She liked the way his fringe flopped forward, slightly hiding his eyes.

'I, um, could do with some experience in retail,' she said. 'This place seemed ideal, especially as you stock such varied clothes. I've shopped here before and some of the vintage stuff is amazing.'

Ben glanced down at his checked shirt and blue jeans. 'Hmm, my sister's always saying I should take more interest in what I wear but I like to keep things simple. If I see a shirt I like, I'll just buy the same one in several different colours. Anyway, you might feel differently about the old stuff, once you see it first in, smelling musty and needing an iron.'

Shoulders less tense, now, Nicky laughed. 'So, um, have you worked here long?' she said.

Ben shrugged. 'Almost nine months. Like you, I started helping out voluntarily, in the sixth form. When I finished my GCEs last summer, a temporary paid position came up, to cover maternity leave - I'm taking a gap year before uni, to go travelling. Trish is due back in a couple of months, by which time I'll have saved up enough for a few months touring the Far East. That's always been my dream...' He grinned. 'Anyway – enough about me.' He pointed out a few items. 'As you can see, we accept almost any type of donations...'

She followed Ben around the shop, as he explained how they arranged the books and DVDs and chose particular ornaments to go on display. He was a bit of a joker, pretending to drop a porcelain cup and trying on a feathered, ladies hat.

'Geoff is retired and helps out once a week,' said Ben. 'He's always been interested in antiques and is great at recognizing and pricing valuable items.' He picked up a tea caddy. On the front was a hand-painted picture of an elephant, a tassled blanket across its back.

'Do you know how to tell this is an Indian elephant?' said Ben. 'Its ears…'

'…turn forwards at the top,' she replied. 'An African elephant's turn backwards.'

Ben's eyes widened. 'I'm impressed.'

'Also an Indian elephant has four toenails on its hind feet, whereas an African has only three.' Nicky grinned. 'My brain seems wired to store useless facts. You know… The kind of things you read in a Christmas cracker.'

Ben grinned back, 'Then I'm putting your name down on our team. *The Perfect Pakora* curry house runs a quiz once a month. Me, Jill, Geoff and one of the van drivers, Steve, team up. It's amazing how much trivia you pick up, working in a place like this. Did you know that around fifty per cent of homes in Britain own a Scrabble set? Not that people often donate such classic games. They hold on to them to play with their kids, and then their grandchildren.'

'Did *you* know that during World War II, maps and money were secretly hidden in Monopoly sets to help prisoners of war escape?' said Nicky.

'No. Wow - you're good.' Ben gave her the thumbs up. 'Promise me you'll pencil our next quiz night into your diary. It's a week on Monday.'

'Oh… Um….'

'The curry house does a mean Chicken Tikka,' said Ben. 'And their speciality is to die for – it's a chilli naan bread.'

Nicky grinned. 'How can I refuse an exotic invitation like that?'

'You absolutely can't,' he said.

They gazed at each other and just for a second, Nicky's stomach tingled.

He cleared his throat. 'Right, anyway…You're interested in fashion, so… Why don't you revamp that window display? Sometimes I dress that dummy, but I haven't much of a clue and just grab the nearest dress or top and trousers. It would be great to finally have someone on board who knows what they are doing.'

Nicky nodded, just staring a moment longer at his warm chocolate eyes. Then she shook herself as a couple of customers came in. Right. Work. The reason she was here… Nicky gazed at the dummy. She could do this. When she hadn't any money to spend, she'd often stand outside boutiques and mentally work out how she'd improve the displays.

Firstly she stripped off the clothes and hung them back on the rails. Then she flicked through the hangars and picked out a flowing cherry dress. Draped over the rail was a gorgeous black knitted cardigan, with ornate buttons. Someone must have forgotten to hang it up properly. Nicky shook her head. It was amazing to see what lovely items some people threw out.

'How's it going?' said Ben, a while later, and passed her a mug of steaming coffee. He'd asked her to keep one eye on the till, whilst he'd nipped out the back. Nicky jerked her head towards the window and the dummy, wearing the cherry dress and black cardigan. Nicky had also found some long black beads in the jewellery cabinet which just finished off the outfit nicely. Outside a woman, in a beret, stared through the window, before coming in to examine the black cardigan. Ben's brow furrowed.

'Where did you find that?' he asked Nicky, in a low voice.

'The cardigan? Um… it was draped over one of the clothes' rails. Why?'

'It's Jill's!' he hissed. 'She took it off this morning and must have forgotten to take it with her.'

Nicky's mouth went dry. Oh no. If she sold her boss's cardigan she'd never be asked back again, to help out. This job was her only chance of getting retail experience with clothes, to help her stand out in the interview, for the course she so badly wanted to study.

'How much is this?' asked the woman in the beret and fingered the sleeve of the cardigan.

Ben opened his mouth to speak, but just at that moment the phone rang and with a strange expression on his face, he hurried over to the till, to answer it. Nicky swallowed hard. 'Um… Fifteen pounds,' she guessed and urgently cast her eye over the rail. Urgh! Why had she said that? She should have straightaway told the lady the truth – but then she would have made the shop look highly unprofessional. Palms feeling sweaty, Nicky gazed at the rails. Whilst looking through earlier, she had spotted a red shrug that would also compliment that dress. She dashed to the till, to put down her drink and then returned to the lady.

'This would also go well,' she said, a small wobble in her voice, as she lifted the tiny red shrug into the air. But the woman took off her beret and shook her head, her grey bobbed hair swinging from side to side.

'It's to go with a pair of black trousers I've just bought for work, dear. And this cardigan is exactly the right length.

'But, um, a contrasting colour could be good,' said Nicky and prayed that Jill wouldn't come back, just then. She stared at the woman's blue eyes, which reminded her of an azure jumper she'd seen. Quickly, Nicky rummaged through the rail and pulled out the small, brand-new looking garment. 'Nowadays black can be an, um, overrated colour. This one would brighten your outfit up and it matches the lovely colour of your eyes.'

The woman blushed. 'That's kind of you to say, dear. Do you really think this jumper would work?'

As a matter of fact, Nicky did. The black cardigan was far too harsh for the woman's very pale complexion. And the jumper fitted perfectly, cinching neatly in at the waist. Plus not one part of it looked second-hand. Exhaling, as the woman agreed to buy it, Nicky led her to the till. Ben was off the phone now.

'Nice sales technique,' he muttered, as the customer left the shop. 'Look, Nicky-'

At that moment Jill returned and shaking her damp umbrella, she stumbled into the shop, out of the blustery shower.

'Goodness, it's blowing a gale outside, now,' she said. 'So, how are things going?' she put her brolly and handbag on the cash-desk and took off her Mackintosh.

Huh? Nicky stared. Jill was wearing a thick, cream jumper.

'Everything all right?' said Jill and looked down at herself, before giving a chuckle. 'Not the prettiest thing, is it? This jumper belongs to my husband - I keep it in the car for especially cold days. I never normally need jumpers in here, unless it's snowing, but after visiting our other branch, I needed warming up. The plumbing problem meant they had to cut off the electrics. It was like a freezer in there!'

Nicky glanced at Ben's whose cheeks burned bright purple.

'That's a great window display, by the way Nicky,' she said. 'That black jumper only came in this morning – it was so gorgeous, I brought it straight out and have a nasty feeling I didn't even price it up. It looks great with that dress – I can tell you're going to be a real asset to the shop. If you want to come back again, that is...' Jill smiled. 'Now, who's for a cuppa?' She picked up her handbag and disappeared into the back room.

Nicky raised one eyebrow at Ben.

'Urgh, sorry, what a fool I am - it was just my little joke.' Ben smiled sheepishly. 'The phone rang, just as I was about to tell you it wasn't actually Jill's cardigan.'

A giggle welled up, inside Nicky's chest. Working here was going to be fun.

'Talk about unprofessional,' she said, stiffly. 'I don't think I'll be coming back to help again.'

'Really? I mean, I'd understand, but I thought you could take a joke, you see...' He gave a sigh. 'You can't leave, Nicky. We need you on our quiz team!'

She giggled.

'Oh, ha ha! Touché.' Ben chuckled, chocolate eyes bright again. Playfully, he punched Nicky on the shoulder, before returning to the till.

Still giggling, she turned to the clothes rails, having already decided on a plan to reorganise them into sections of colour.

'Nicky?' said Ben, ten minutes later. He was heading over to her, an arm around a gentleman's shoulder. 'This is Mr Morris, one of our most loyal regulars. He's looking for something smart. Perhaps you could-'

'Leave it to me,' she said and smiled at the elderly man, as Ben returned to the till. 'Somewhere I've seen a nicely tailored waistcoat that's just your size,' said Nicky. Ooh, she'd always fancied being a personal shopper! 'Then we could take a look through the tie rack...'

The man nodded enthusiastically.

As she caught Ben's eye, across the shop, he gave her a wink. Cheeks hot, Nicky smiled and had the feeling that Gran had been right. Volunteering here would not only help her achieve her career goals, but also spice up her life – especially if she was going to join Ben on that quiz team and try that chilli naan bread!

2
BIRDS OF A FEATHER

Billy kicked a pebble as the bus pulled away. Then he and Alf walked ahead of Charles and Joan - *the parents*. Not that Uncle Charlie was Billy's dad - he belonged to Alf. No one could ever replace Billy's beloved "Pa" who was shot in Belgian woodland, at the end of 1944.

Billy would never forget Ma's sobbing, even though it was almost three years ago, when he was ten. Billy sighed. The last month had been hard, since Uncle Charlie had been coming around more often, with fourteen year old Alf. He'd done his best to avoid talking to them by taking out his Beano comics, or switching on the wireless, whenever they called. He and Alf had once had a good game of marbles, but Billy would never admit to having enjoyed that.

'Lads!' called Uncle Charlie. 'Stop for a moment. Can you hear that?'

As the two boys ground to a halt, the breeze carried the distinctive call of a cuckoo.

'Perhaps we'll spot one,' said Uncle Charlie as he approached, Ma on his arm in her straw hat. 'Look out for a bird with a grey head and upper body. The belly is white with black stripes.' The man glanced at Billy and gave a half-smile. 'Have you ever seen one, lad?'

Billy shrugged and shook his head, hardly making eye contact. Uncle Charlie's mouth drooped at the corners and

Ma squeezed his arm.

'Don't they lay their eggs in other birds' nests?' said Alf.

'That's right, son,' said Uncle Charlie. 'When the big chick hatches, it pushes out the others belonging to its new mother.'

Billy smirked as he and the older boy ambled ahead. The parents had sat on a bench and were gazing at the forest view. As the two boys made their way to the placid lake, Billy glanced sideways at Alf.

'You remind me of a baby Cuckoo,' he muttered and smirked again.

'Huh?' said Alf as they sat down by the water's edge.

'What with you getting our old lodger's big bedroom, once Uncle Charlie's divorce is through, and you move in. It should be mine.'

'But I'm the eldest.'

'Only by a year,' said Billy. 'And it's not even your home.'

Alf plucked a handful of grass. 'Like it or not, Billy, it will be one day.'

'Yeah, only cos your mum's going off to America...'

'So? Brad's okay. He always got me chewing gum and Nylons for Mum.' Alf's voice gave a wobble. 'Dad was missing in action for so long, everyone thought he was dead. Even the army – until they realized there'd been a mix-up.'

'I wish the French Resistance had sheltered my Pa,' muttered Billy. Life wasn't fair. But then he had to admit, it wasn't fair for Alf to be told his dad was dead, when he wasn't. 'So, why don't you go over the ocean with her?'

Alf's cheeks blotched red. 'Wish I was, some days, but Dad's boss says there's a job for me at the factory, when I leave school, and… I've some missed years to make up, with Dad. Mum and Brad say I'm welcome to join them, any time I want…' Alf shrugged. 'Brad's good for Mum - made her smile again; taught her to jitterbug. Mum's eyes had been red for weeks, before he came along.'

Billy swallowed hard as he pictured his ma's bright face, every time she opened the front door to Uncle Charlie. She'd giggle like a teenager, a rare sound since they'd got the telegram about Pa.

The frown on his head more relaxed, Billy stared at Alf. 'Yeah, well, even when you're living with us, I'll never call your father "dad".'

Alf picked up a pebble and lobbed it into the sunlit water, ahead. 'That's the last thing he'd expect, after living with his own stepdad.'

Billy raised his eyebrows.

'My grandpa died when Dad was ten – something to do with his heart. Dad said it meant hard times for Gran and she thought it was best to quickly marry again…'

So Uncle Charlie had lost his father at the same age Billy lost his. Billy glanced back at Alf's dad, trying to imagine him as a boy.

'…But her second husband liked his beer,' continued Alf. 'He'd threaten to belt the stepchildren if they refused to call him "Father".'

Billy turned back around and wiped some mud off his shorts. He could never imagine softly-spoken Uncle Charlie doing that.

The cuckoo called again.

'Stupid birds,' mumbled Billy, still determined not to enjoy any attempt at a family day out.

Alf's eyes crinkled at the corners. 'Then why did I catch you looking through Dad's bird-watching manual last time you visited us?' He stood up. 'Let's skim stones.'

Alf bent down to choose a flat one and threw it across the water. It bounced two times. Billy's stone did the same. Shirt sleeves rolled up, Uncle Charlie came over and his managed three bounces.

'My dad once did five,' said Billy, and puffed out his chest.

'So your mum was just telling me.' Uncle Charlie smiled. 'I don't think I'll ever achieve that.' Suddenly he cocked his head. 'Let's go around the lake, towards the forest. I'm sure I heard a woodpecker. Here, Billy… Why don't you take my binoculars?'

Billy looked Uncle Charlie in the eye. 'Um… Yeah. Okay. Thanks.'

The grown-ups trailed behind, whilst the two boys headed towards the forest.

'If you like…' said Alf, uncertainly, '… we can go to the sweetshop when we get back.'

'Ma's used our last coupon,' said Billy, 'to buy chocolate for my aunt's birthday last week.

Alf grinned. 'Good thing I beat Bertie Green at arm wrestling, then! He gave me his.'

'But the shops don't take loose coupons.'

'Apparently Mr Butler on Eaves Avenue does,' said Alf in a low voice. 'Bertie says he sells decent toffees.'

'S'pose you'll, um, want something in return, then,' said Billy. 'Guess you could borrow my train set, next time you call. We could set it up in the old lodger's room. There's not enough space for it in my bedroom, anyway, since Uncle Charlie made me that extra track.'

'Boys!' hissed Uncle Charlie. 'Up there!' He pointed to the top of a conifer tree.

Gazing through the binoculars, Billy followed the

tree's trunk to the top. Sure enough, to the left, was a red-headed bird, pecking the bark. He passed the binoculars to Alf.

'That small beak sure can make a loud noise,' said Billy.

'A bit like your crying when you were younger.' Ma smiled. 'It was louder than the air-raid sirens!'

'But less painful than Alf on his harmonica,' replied Billy.

Uncle Charlie chuckled.

'You'd better be nice if you want some sweets, squirt,' said Alf, eyes twinkling, as they walked on.

'Who are you calling squirt?' said Billy. 'Pa was a giant of a man so I'll overtake you in height, one day.'

'I'll always be faster, though. Race you to that turnstile,' said Alf and pointed in the distance. Alf counted down from ten and then they were off.

Chest heaving, Billy stared ahead at the older boy. Before today, he hadn't really thought about his stepbrother-to-be missing his own mum. Plus, at one point Alf thought his dad was dead, and Billy knew how bad that felt. Maybe, just maybe, they had more in common than he'd originally thought...

'Right behind you, Alf!' Billy hollered and leapt over a molehill. Spurred on by his ma's cheers, he sped forwards.

3

THE PERFECT PANCAKE

An expectant smile across her face, Tricia stood in the primary school playground. Everyone was waiting for the Going Home bell. Other mums chatted over prams, as if this was just another ordinary afternoon, which to them, it probably was - but not for Tricia. She'd been looking forward to today for ages. Having been owed time in lieu, she'd been allowed home early enough, from work, to do the school run. For once, Tricia was determined to be one of those domestic superwomen - like Grace's mum.

Today Grace was coming to tea. It was Shrove Tuesday and Tricia was out to impress. First of all they would make pancakes, then she'd found instructions on the internet to make cute papier-mâché piggy banks. As for tea, Tricia's daughter, Amy, said they often had chicken and potatoes at Grace's house, so even though it was mid-week, Tricia was preparing a roast.

A woman in a smart tailored coat and beret walked over.

'Hello... Tricia, isn't it? We had a quick chat at the Christmas Fair – over the chocolate tombola.' She smiled.

'Um...'

'I'm Debs. My daughter's in Mrs Taylor's class, too. She's called Emma.'

'Of course,' said Tricia and blushed, feeling decidedly frumpy next to this fashion plate. Yet, now she remembered Debs from the fair – how she'd made Tricia laugh and given Amy a chocolate bar.

'How are you settling in? Amy really must come around for tea, sometime, before time flies even quicker and our daughters are at high school.' Debs grinned.

'Thank you. I'm sure she'd love that.' Tricia smiled. 'Christmas seems so long ago, now. I can't believe it's already February.'

'Is Amy enjoying school?' asked Debs, as the bell went. 'And how about you? It must be hard, what with you working and...' Her voice petered out.

'Amy's very happy, thanks. But yes, it's a shame I can't pick her up more often. Although it's strange, moving back here and re-visiting the school I attended as a child.'

'Did you, really?' The woman's jaw dropped. 'Goodness, I can't imagine living where I grew up, although... Needs must, I suppose. And of course, this is a lovely spot to bring up children. Well, nice to see you again, Tricia...' She smiled awkwardly, and went to meet her daughter, as children began to file out of classrooms.

Needs must? Tricia gave a wry smile. That was one way of putting it. Since Nick had died in a car crash two years ago, it had been hard managing by herself. Eventually, last autumn she'd moved back to her childhood village, and her parents, who'd been brilliant helping Amy cope with the loss of her dad.

'Mum!' Amy ran up to Tricia, brunette curls bouncing, a proud smile on her face. The little girl glanced sideways, as if secretly hoping everyone in the world – or playground, at least - would notice who was picking her up, today.

'Hello, darling!' Tricia bent over and gave her a big hug. 'Where's Grace?'

Amy pointed to her friend who stood by the classroom doorway, chatting with the teacher.

'How was your maths test?' asked Tricia.

'It went okay.'

'And what did you have for lunch?'

'My favourite trifle for pud!' she said, eyes shining, all green with chestnut speckles, just like her father's.

'Yum!' Tricia smiled.

'Are me and Grace still making pancakes?' asked Amy.

'Of course. The milk, flour and eggs are waiting.'

'Goody! It was fab making them at Grace's house, last time I was there. Her mum let me have chocolate spread. It was the perfect pancake.' She took Tricia's hand and smiled cheekily. 'Can I have two?'

'We'll see!'

Grace's mum, Jo, did a lot of things that Amy thought were 'fab'. Like making doll furniture out of cardboard, doing treasure-hunts and cooking pancakes, whether or not it was Shrove Tuesday. Tricia had hardly got to know Jo, herself, because when picking up Amy, she was always in such a rush to get back for the homework, bath and bed routine. In fact, the last two years seemed to have passed by like a movie reel on fast-forward.

Tricia bit her lip. What was she like? Things could be a lot worse. At least Mum and Dad helped out with childcare and she should be grateful that a generous mum like Jo had welcomed Amy into the village, with such open arms.

'Here we are,' said Tricia, in a bright voice, as they passed some holly bushes and reached her modest cottage. How lovely it had been, strolling with the two girls and chatting to them about their busy day. 'Brr, there's already frost sparkling on the pavement. Let's get in and I'll put the heating on. What a good thing you two are wearing your scarves.'

'Mum knitted mine,' said Grace, as they stood in the hall way.

'Isn't she clever?' said Tricia and smiled as she hung up their coats.

The girls went into the kitchen, to be greeted by the smell of roasting meat. They washed their hands, then stood expectantly in the kitchen, hovering by the mixing bowl that Tricia had set out, after racing back from the office to put the chicken on.

'Why do we have a Pancake Day?' said Amy, as Grace messily sifted flour into the bowl.

'It's the last chance to eat the yummy foods that were traditionally cut out during Lent,' she said.

'Lent?' chorused the girls.

'It's a religious festival, where people fast for forty days. Fasting means not eating – or, at least, not eating a lot.'

'Yikes. I wouldn't be very good at that,' said Amy, in a serious tone.

Tricia smiled. 'Nowadays, a lot of people just give up their favourite treats, instead.'

'Like sweets?' said Grace.

Tricia nodded.

'I could try that, Mum! Think of all the pocket money I'd save.'

Tricia smiled and ruffled her daughter's hair.

The girls broke one egg each, into the flour, and shell shattered everywhere. With giggles they picked out the broken bits. Then Tricia poured in the milk and Amy and Grace took it in turns to whisk the batter.

'That mixture looks lovely and smooth, now,' said

Tricia, and carefully heated a knob of butter in a small pan. She let Amy pour in some batter and then closely supervised, as Grace prodded the first pancake whilst it fried.

It was years since Tricia had made pancakes, since they'd always been Nick's forte. In fact one of the first home-made meals he'd wooed her with, was savoury pancakes, stuffed with ricotta and spinach. Tricia reckoned a man who could cook like that, would make an excellent husband and he'd proved her right. She smiled to herself. Nick used to take his cookery extremely seriously, so one Christmas she bought him a white chef's hat. He wore it during the turkey dinner, instead of the gold crown out of his cracker.

'Can we toss the pancake, Mummy?' said Amy.

'Um…'

'Please, Mrs Hart!' said Grace.

'Okay…' Tricia smiled nervously. 'You first, Grace – but let's do it well away from the hob, over this wooden chopping board.'

Grace nodded excitedly and moved to the right. She jerked the pan upwards. Nothing. The pancake wouldn't budge.

'Oh dear, it's stuck – perhaps I didn't put in enough butter,' said Tricia as she scraped the mixture off the bottom of the pan. 'Let's try once more.'

Which they did, and again, until finally a pancake flipped but landed on the floor. Another landed on the worktop and the last in the nearby sink. Between the three of them, they hadn't made one decent pancake, before all the mixture was gone. Tricia couldn't believe it and shook her head.

'Can we make more batter, Mummy?' said Amy.

'No, sorry, darling, I need the rest of the flour to make glue for papier-mâché piggy banks.'

'Papier-mâché? Yay!' said Amy and clapped her hands, the disastrous cookery session already forgotten. Just like her dad, she was a glass half-full kind of person, who rarely saw the negatives. Like when Tricia lost her wedding ring, after ten years of marriage - Nick said never mind, they could now afford to buy a better one and use it as an excuse to renew their vows. He would have chuckled at Tricia's attempts at pancake-making. How she missed their teasing of each other and a grin flickered briefly across her face, as she recalled how he had a real talent for killing any houseplant. Whilst Nick could cook, he'd concede that Tricia was the one with green fingers.

She cleared the kitchen table, set out a pile of newspapers and blew up two balloons. Time was ticking and Tricia still had vegetables to prepare for tea. Grace was being picked up at six.

'Right,' she said, one eye on the clock, 'these balloons are the body of the pig, girls. You need to cover them with the special glue and torn up bits of newspaper.' Quickly she mixed up the flour and water. It was simple enough. She didn't need to check the internet instructions.

Except that for some reason the paste was too runny, so she double-checked after all. Aarggh! She'd used twice the amount of water necessary and now had no extra flour, to thicken it up. Not that the girls were bothered, they were giggling too much at how slimy the glue felt. Reluctantly, they washed their hands and then, still laughing, charged off to play Amy's video games.

Tricia shook her head. It was no good. She'd never be one of those domestic goddesses. She opened the oven door and peered in at the golden chicken. At least she made a decent roast. Perhaps Grace's mum would be impressed with that.

'Tea's ready!' she eventually called and footsteps pounded as the girls ran downstairs and into the kitchen. Grace stopped and stared at her plate, before sitting down. Her bottom lip quivered.

'Everything all right?' said Tricia. 'Eat up girls – I'm running late. Your mum will be here in fifteen minutes, Grace.'

Grace picked up a fork and moved some peas around her plate. Tricia raised her eyebrows. 'Don't you like it?' she said, gently. 'Amy, I thought you said you had chicken and potatoes at Grace's house.'

'We do,' said Amy, in between mouthfuls, 'but they're not like this.'

'Sorry, Mrs Hart,' said Grace, shyly.

'All right, poppet,' said Tricia and scolded herself mentally for not having checked with Amy exactly what "chicken and potatoes" meant. On the few occasions she'd had Grace over before, during the odd holiday week, she'd played it safe with fish fingers and chips or burgers. Perhaps she should have done that, again. 'How about a cheese sandwich?' she said.

Five minutes later, the little guest was tucking into cheddar on white bread, just as the doorbell rang. Wiping her hands on a tea-towel, Tricia went into the hallway. She took a deep breath and opened the door.

'Hello, Jo,' she said. 'Come on in - the girls are still finishing tea.'

Peals of laughter rang through, from the kitchen.

'They sound like they're having fun,' said Jo and grinned. 'I hope Grace has behaved herself.'

'It's always a pleasure to have her over,' said Tricia. 'I

just wish I could manage it more often.'

Jo followed her through the lounge, into the kitchen.

'Hi Mum!' said Grace and took a bite of her sandwich.

Tricia looked sheepish and put down the tea towel. 'I thought Amy had eaten chicken and potatoes like this, at yours, Jo, but I must have got it wrong. Grace didn't want the roast.'

'Urgh! Sorry. I should have mentioned that my daughter isn't a huge fan of vegetables – try as I may! Her favourite meal is chicken nuggets and potato wedges. That's probably what I've given Amy, in the past.' Jo kissed Grace on the head and then glanced around at the dirty pots and pans. 'What a shame, after you went to so much trouble.'

'We made pancakes, Mum!' said Grace, before slurping down the rest of her squash and starting on her fruit salad.

'Well, we tried to…' said Tricia and pointed to the remnants of burnt batter, in the small frying pan, by the sink.

Jo chuckled. 'Remember what happened when we made them at ours, girls?'

Amy giggled. 'One stuck to the ceiling.'

'And the batter was all lumpy,' said Grace.

'Really?' said Tricia. Her daughter hadn't told her that. She'd said the pancakes were perfect.

'In the end I dashed out and bought some from the corner shop,' said Jo and laughed. 'Now, they *were* tasty – plus nicely round and not burnt.'

'Can we finish our video game?' said Amy. 'It won't take long. Pleeassssseee!'

Tricia glanced at the girls' empty fruit salad bowls. 'Well, I don't mind… Um, Jo, is that okay? Would you like

26

a quick coffee?'

'That would be great.' Jo took off her coat and grinned. 'But you'll have to excuse my jumper.'

Tricia hung the coat over a chair and glanced at Jo's top. The neck was baggy and the arms way too long.

'It's just for skulking around the house in,' said Jo. 'I took up knitting last year and have just about mastered scarves – taking on a jumper was a bit too ambitious.'

Tricia's shoulders relaxed as she switched on the kettle. Jo should see her sewing! Straight seams weren't her strong point. Perhaps they could swap notes on clothes-making disasters!

'Um, Jo… I haven't had time to say before,' said Tricia, 'but I really appreciate how often you've had Amy over. She loves spending time at your house. Last week's treasure hunt sounded fun. You must haves spent ages organising it.'

Jo's cheeks tinged pink. 'Didn't Amy tell you exactly what they were hunting for?'

Tricia's brow furrowed.

'My car keys – as usual, I lost them. The, um, treasure was a packet of chewy sweets, for whoever found them.'

'Oh…' Tricia grinned. 'Well, she loved that card making you helped them with, at Christmas. I tried papier-mâché with the girls, tonight, but the glue turned out too runny.'

'The things us mums do, eh? And hats off to you, it's difficult enough fitting everything in, when you're at home all day, let alone…' She glanced at Tricia. 'Look, you should team up with me and Debs – you know, Emma's mum?'

Tricia raised an eyebrow and took out two mugs.

'We've decided to start going to the cinema once a

fortnight, in town,' continued Jo. 'It's a starting point, for regaining some sort of social life. I was on the phone to Debs, just before I came over here – she mentioned bumping into you, in the playground, and wondered if you'd like to come along to see a film, too.'

'Oh... that's kind. She seems very nice. Her, um, dress-sense puts me to shame.'

'Just before you moved here, she'd spent a year losing almost four stone. Debs had never got rid of her baby weight and used to live in jogging suits.'

Tricia gasped. 'Goodness. You'd never guess.'

'I know. Now she looks as if she's stepped out of a catalogue – a far cry from me and my knitted jumpers!' She smiled. 'So, how about it? We're going on our first cinema trip next week.'

Tricia cleared the table of the girls' plates and put down two mugs of coffee, the milk jug and sugar bowl. She sat opposite Jo.

'I'd love to go out, now and again, but to be honest, I don't like to impose any more on my parents. They've been so good, picking Amy up from school every day, and looking after her until I'm back from the office, but they've got their own lives, too. I don't want to take advantage – even though I know they wouldn't see it like that.'

'I understand,' said Jo, softly. 'It's a lot easier for me and Debs... But wait a minute – my niece, Jess, she's in the sixth form, and is desperate to save money for college. She's been babysitting over the last year. Why doesn't Amy come to tea next Monday and I could invite Jess over? You could both meet her. She's looked after my Grace and her younger brother often enough, and has turned out unbelievably sensible...' Jo's eyes twinkled. '...

despite her obsession with at least five boy bands!'

Tricia sipped her coffee. A social life? That was an exciting prospect!

'Her rates are very reasonable - especially if you throw in a large packet of crisps.' Jo grinned.

'Okay – thanks,' said Tricia. 'I'd really appreciate that.'

'Jess also makes the perfect pancake.' Eyes twinkling, Jo pulled a face. 'Unlike us imperfect mums.'

Tricia's chest glowed. Whether they went out to work or not, she guessed that most mums had a lot in common - like trying to do their best for their kids; like worrying too much when not always succeeding.

'What's this film about?' she asked.

'It's a romance - based in a patisserie,' said Jo. 'Who knows…? Maybe it'll teach you and me something about dessert-making.'

Tricia caught her eye and Amy and Grace came running in, and looked quizzically at their mums. Tricia winked at Amy and decided that despite the burnt pancakes, the afternoon couldn't have gone better.

4
FAR FROM THE TREE

Mouth down-turned, Tim shrugged at Andy, his dad. What had been the point in even asking? As if there was any chance his parents would buy him a new souped-up phone, like that of Josh, his best friend. Just this once, Tim would have liked to keep up with his pal's gadgets, instead of always being the last to get the latest computer game. He still hadn't got his own laptop.

Tim sighed and told himself not to act spoilt. Mum and Dad were right – "things" didn't matter, it was what was inside that counted. Except Josh seemed to have it all and they weren't even at High School until next year - a flat-screen telly in his room, cool computer, amazing digital camera and "smart" phone (whatever that was).

Josh had moved to Tim's school six months ago, when his dad changed jobs, and immediately the two boys had hit it off. Not only did Josh own all the latest technical devices, he was also very generous and let Tim play with them all.

'Perhaps at Christmas we'll review updating your phone,' said Mum. 'I'll ask Santa.'

'Very funny, Mum,' said Tim and rolled his eyes. He thought about a phrase that Gran sometimes said - that "the apple didn't fall far from the tree." In other words, she reckoned he was a lot like Dad. Like when he brought back a praised piece of artwork from school, or won at a board game (Dad was mad on Scrabble).

He sighed. Gran had got it wrong. As falling apples went, Tim reckoned a gust of wind must have carried him into distant fields, cos unlike Dad, Tim liked cool cars, modern televisions and designer trainers - like Josh's.

Mum smiled. 'Okay, failing Santa, who knows? Perhaps there'll be some deals on, at work.'

Tim grunted. Maybe. Sometimes it was handy, her working at the huge, out-of-town supermarket. With a sigh, he gave a small smile and tried to understand why he always had to wait for new stuff. Unlike Josh's sleek family car, theirs had had two previous owners and was starting to rust. Plus Mum often darned holes in clothes. He could never imagine Josh's poshly dressed parents doing that.

Mum shook her head. 'In any case, Josh has only just turned eleven – it's ridiculous him owning such a fancy phone, at that age.'

'Well, his dad's job in the city pays loads,' said Tim and glanced at Andy. 'Not that... Well, you know - Dad's pottery shop is great.'

Andy ruffled his son's hair. 'Look, why don't you invite Josh around next week? You can paint the ceramic mugs you both made, in my workshop, last Monday.'

Tim's face brightened. 'That would be good. Like last time, can we go to the park afterwards? You were such a cool goalie cos you let all the shots past!'

'Cheeky monkey!' Andy chuckled. 'Of course - as long as I'm on target with my latest order, if I get it. The Coffee Cup café, in town, rang today. It's had a makeover and the owner, Mrs Bradshaw, wants to meet up to discuss me producing a selection of ornamental mugs and wall-plates, embossed with their new logo.'

'Cool!' said Tim, although sometimes, secretly, he couldn't help wishing Dad had a more flash job. Then they could go skiing, like Josh did. Plus his pal was off to America, visiting Disneyworld, this summer.

'The Coffee Cup? Sounds exciting, well done, love,' said Mum. 'Although don't forget, it's Dad's Day at the school next Friday. You mustn't miss that. It's the last one, what with Tim leaving Junior school, at the end of this term.'

'I wouldn't miss it for the world – it's marked on my calendar in capitals,' said Andy. 'We had great fun last year building that model Merry-Go-Round.'

Dad's Day was held every year, at Tim's primary school. On the Friday before Father's Day's, dads were invited for the afternoon. They would be given a project to complete with their children, in the classroom. It was also a great opportunity for those grown-ups, who weren't often in the playground, to get to know each other.

Soon enough, that Friday came around – a bright and breezy June day. Towards the end of lunchtime, all the children gazed at the school gates, whooping and waving madly as, one by one, their dads appeared - whereas Josh seemed kind of downcast, as if his favourite football team had just lost.

'I'm sure he'll make it, Josh,' said Tim.

'Dunno.' The disheartened boy shrugged. 'He said something about an important meeting.'

'But look, there he is!' Tim pointed to the school gates.

Josh's face broke into a smile as he spotted a man, in a sharp Italian suit, rushing in last, still talking non-stop on his phone. Fifteen minutes later, the dads filed into the classrooms, following afternoon register.

'Hi, Mr Smith!' chimed several of Tim's friends, as they

saw Andy, who wore brown cords and a T-shirt which said "Keep Calm and Potter Around" – a present from his wife, the previous Christmas. Tim's chest glowed as his dad greeted various boys, by name. Over the years many of his pals had visited to make pottery or have tea. In fact, his dad's "Cowboy's Dinner" of sausages with beans, gravy and mash was legendary!

'How are you, Ryan,' said Andy and smiled at a red-haired, freckled lad. 'Is that piggy bank you made at ours, still in one piece?'

Ryan blushed almost as red as his hair. Andy chuckled.

'Only teasing, son – I bumped into your mum, last week. She told me you'd accidentally dropped it on the tiled kitchen floor, and it smashed. Come around soon and we'll make another.'

Tim grinned at Ryan who nodded vigorously.

'Mr Smith, did you manage to fix your kiln,' asked a boy with a wide gap between his front teeth. He knew Andy well because he helped out at Scouts.

'Hi, Callum,' said Andy. 'Sure did. The problem was to do with something inside called the element – I'll show you, next time you visit. I bought a new one and managed to replace it myself.'

'Wow, that's amazing,' said Callum.

Andy and Tim exchanged a humorous look. It hadn't been a straightforward job and Tim had kept his dad supplied with orange squash. To celebrate a job well done, when Mum got home from work, she baked dad's favourite carrot cake.

Andy smiled at Josh, who hovered nearby. 'Have you finished celebrating shooting all those goals past me, the other night?'

Briefly Josh's eyes crinkled at the corners, before he stared, once again into the school corridor. Tim's eyes followed. Marcus was chatting away on his mobile, the only dad who still hadn't come into the classroom. Perhaps having a swanky phone wasn't so good after all.

Finally Marcus slipped his mobile into his pocket and hurried in.

He clapped Josh on the back. 'Afternoon, sonny. Hi there, Tim. So, what's this all about?'

'We're going to make an aeroplane, out of a squash bottle, chopsticks, lids and toilet rolls!' said Josh, his brow now smoothed out.

Andy held out his hand. 'Hey, Marcus. Long time no see – we must go for another drink, at some point. Your work's still busy, no doubt?'

Marcus shook Andy's hand. 'Don't ask. As the new boy, I'm still working all hours to establish my reputation.' As he chatted about bad traffic, targets and business lunches, Tim noticed the dark rings under the smart man's eyes. His dad never looked like that, but then he didn't work all hours and only had a minute's walk, to reach his "office", as the pottery shop was an extension, built onto their house. He and Mum often mumbled stuff about "quality of life" being important. Maybe that's what they meant.

'Thanks for having Josh over this week, by the way,' continued Marcus. 'How's the pottery shop going? Business booming?'

Andy shrugged. 'Can't complain, mate, although we won't be joining you in Disneyworld, any time soon.'

'At least you're your own boss,' muttered Marcus and grimaced as his fancy phone bleeped.

'*Dad*, you promised, no calls,' hissed Josh.

'Sorry, sonny, won't be a second - I just need to text back,' said Marcus with a sheepish look. He disappeared back into the corridor.

'Come on, lads,' said Andy, to Josh and Tim, in a cheery voice. 'We've got to work together, in a four. Let's grab a table and see if we can't make the best aeroplane ever!'

Just over an hour later, Josh and Tim proudly showed their piece of work, to the teacher. Great effort had been made to construct the fiddly bits, choose the paint colour, plus a catchy name to carefully draw on the side. Marcus's phone had only bleeped once more. Now he stood, fancy jacket off, sleeves rolled up, laughing with Andy. Tim thought how much younger Josh's dad looked, than an hour earlier.

'Good thing we were paired with you, Andy,' said Marcus, as the boys came back. 'Josh is great with his hands but me, well – I've never been the practical sort. His teacher lost me when she explained how to make the fuselage.'

Andy chuckled. 'Well, I'd be equally lost if someone asked me to analyse stocks and shares, like you do, all day, which is a pity – a job like yours might have helped me achieve my childhood dream of owning a sports car, by the time I turned forty!'

'Dad's brill at maths,' said Josh, proudly.

'I let Tim's Mum help out with that,' said Andy and grinned. 'Art was always my strong point, at school. The maths teacher used to despair of me, doodling in his lessons.'

Tim stared at Dad, trying to imagine him as a boy, fantasizing about owning a fast car, just like he did. Could Gran be a tiny bit right about Tim not falling so far from the tree?

The teacher announced that refreshments were now being served in the playground. Thirsty from the afternoon's challenges, the children and dads made their way outside, laughing and chatting.

'Sorry, sonny – gotta dash,' said Marcus.

Josh put on a brave smile, his throat bulging as he swallowed hard. 'S'okay, Dad. Mum said you might have to leave early – at least you made it for the main bit.'

Tim stared at his friend and wondered if he looked like that, every time Mum and Dad said they couldn't afford new stuff. Maybe things weren't so different for him and his pal as neither felt their life was perfect – Tim wanted more "things", whereas Josh wanted more time with his dad.

He glanced across Andy who, as usual, was making the other boys laugh and decided, given the choice, he'd rather have his life than Josh's.

'I'll ring you about the camping, Marcus,' called Andy and winked at Josh's dad who gave a quick wave.

'Huh?' said Tim, as Marcus left.

Josh raised his eyebrows.

'Us two dads reckon a weekend away camping, just us four, might be good fun,' said Andy.

'Really?' said Josh, eyes suddenly sparkling. 'When?'

'At the end of July – just before you go to Disneyworld.'

'Yay!' said Tim. 'We can barbecue sausages and toast marshmallows like we did in Cornwall, camping with Mum.'

'I've never been in a tent before,' said Josh.

'Ours is big enough for all of us,' said Andy and grinned as Josh hurried away to tell this exciting news to another friend.

'Sorry, Tim, but this camping trip might be your only holiday this year,' said Andy. 'The kiln's been playing up again, plus we'll soon need a new car.'

'Doesn't matter, Dad. In fact… I've been thinking – don't worry about a new phone. I can manage with the one I've got.'

'You're a good lad.' Andy ruffled Tim's hair. 'Anyway, we'll have our usual fun during the holidays – cooking, working in the shop together…'

'Me beating you at board games,' said Tim and they both laughed as they headed out into the sunshine. The boy glanced sideways at his father who stopped by a table and picked up two apples. He passed one to Tim.

'Dad…How come you never took a job that would get you that sports car you wanted?'

Andy shrugged. 'I soon worked out that I'd rather spend time with my family, and do something I love all day, instead of having a stressful, unenjoyable career, with long hours.'

Tim nodded and side by side, they headed over to the school benches. Deep in thought, they both sat down and bit into their apples.

5

A RED, RED, ROSE

With a grin, Alistair lightly punched Rose on the shoulder, as if he were her brother - except that he wasn't. Quite simply, they were the best of friends. Rose tired of explaining this to her housemates, Cheryl and Susie, who regularly winked and nudged, convinced that the Scotsman and English girl made the perfect couple.

'Glad you chose to study French, then?' said Alistair, as Rose gave another sigh. They'd just left the university buildings and were heading towards the library. 'Did you keep up with everything, in that lecture?'

Rose pulled a face. 'I wish Professor Petit would speak in English, for once,' she groaned. 'I still can't catch everything he says.'

'Och, don't beat yourself up - we've only been here a term. Everyone says it gets a good deal easier after next year's placement in France. Cheer up, now.' Alistair pulled one of his funny faces that never failed to make Rose laugh.

'That's attractive,' she said and giggled. 'I never knew the Scots were such a handsome race. All I'd heard was that you watched the pennies and loved your deep-fried Mars bars…'

'Dear me, what clichés - next you'll expect me to wear a tartan kilt, you prissy, soft-centred Sassenach,' said Alistair, a comical glint in his eyes.

Rose grinned. She still had no idea what that word meant. He'd called her it ever since they'd met at the Fresher's ball, last autumn. To be fair, she'd been the one to instigate their friendly joshing, by pretending his Scottish accent was incomprehensible. Although secretly, she found his highland lilt very appealing - not that she'd ever let him know that!

As they buttoned up their coats, the teasing morphed into a comfortable silence. They crossed a road, his arm hovering around her shoulders. Normally she'd have grinned and pushed him away, but for once she accepted his over-protectiveness.

'Thinking about home?' she asked, eventually.

'Och, not really.'

'Liar!' she said and they both smiled.

'So, today, the twenty-fifth of January, is Burns Night? Tell me again, how you usually celebrate.' Rose's eyes twinkled. 'Doesn't your dad have to catch and kill a haggis, before your mum gets started on the meal?'

Alistair snorted. 'Ha ha! As if I haven't heard that old myth, before!' He walked around an icy puddle. 'All my cousins visit. Ma cooks haggis, with neeps and tatties. Auntie Moira reads out her favourite Robbie Burns poems. Da drinks too much whiskey and declares his love for everyone.' He shrugged. 'Tradition is important, in my family. Uncle Duncan even gives us a tune, on his bagpipes.'

Rose held open the library door and insisted Alistair go in first. As tall as any man she'd ever met, he ducked his head and went into the warm.

'Is it a difficult instrument to master?' she said and unbuttoned her duffle coat.

'People say it takes seven years and seven generations,

to play bagpipes well. When I was a lad, I had a go and could hardly blow in enough air, to produce one note.'

The librarian stared at them and Alistair winked at Rose. As they parted company, to write their essays, Rose noticed how his shoulders drooped. She could tell he missed the highlands. Perhaps he regretted going so far south to study. She sat down, just as a girl came in, wearing black tights under a tartan mini-skirt.

Of course! That was it! Why didn't she think of this before? How about Rose arranged her very own Burns night for Alistair that celebrated all things Scottish? Surely that would cheer him up. Even better, she would keep it a surprise. She had a tartan scarf that she could probably incorporate into a themed outfit and if she asked nicely, Cheryl and Susie might help her tidy up!

Rose glanced at her watch. It was almost two. She only had one more seminar, at three. That would just give her time to dash into town, afterwards. She reckoned the fancy deli next to the newsagents might sell haggis – or something similar. Then all she had to get was turnips and a small bottle of whiskey. Plus the bargain music shop might sell some CDs of bagpipe music… If it wasn't for the strict librarian, Rose might have clapped her hands in glee.

As she left the library, Rose came to Alistair's desk, smiled at him and thrust a note into his hand, before walking on. It said:

Drop by mine at around seven tonight, if you dare try my cooking! I need to use up some leftovers. We could practise for tomorrow's French interpreting seminar. Hope to see you later!

Okay - so the invitation sounded very casual, but Rose didn't want him to guess that she'd planned something special. Anyway, Alistair had complained all morning that he hadn't enough money to go out for even one pint, that night. She reckoned that - like any student – there was no way he'd miss a free meal. And she hadn't completely misled him – she would be using leftovers, what with the boiled potatoes in the fridge, from when she'd cooked too many for a shepherd's pie.

'So what's this all in aid of, again?' asked Cheryl, late that afternoon, as she helped Rose quickly vacuum the worn, patterned lounge carpet and dust the room.

'Rose wants our house to look its best for that certain someone,' said Susie and giggled in the kitchen, where she was peeling turnips.

'Oh, of course.' Cheryl grinned. 'At last you two lovebirds are getting together!'

'Guys!' said Rose, in an exasperated voice. 'How many times? Alistair is just a good friend.'

'But you always go for tall men,' called through Susie.

'But not dark hair,' said Rose, hotly.

'And you love regional accents,' teased Cheryl. 'That's the only reason you watch Coronation Street.'

'Scottish isn't regional… It's more like a foreign language!' said Rose, determined to prove them wrong on every point.

'Thou doth protesteth too much,' called out Susie. 'When we saw the latest Bond film you said that no actor could beat Sean Connery, as he had the most adorable accent.'

Rose folded her arms, her brow furrowed.

'Oh dear. We'd better stop, Susie,' said Cheryl, in a loud voice. She smiled at Rose. 'Just ignore us. We're only jealous. It's ages since either of us have shared a nice meal, with a man, be him just a good friend or not.'

'Stay if you want,' said Rose and raised her eyebrows.

Cheryl shook her head. 'Thanks, but it's film club night. So, what are you going to wear?'

'Black leggings with my new red jumper. My tartan scarf might act as a belt.' She looked around. 'Talking of which, it's time to get changed. I really appreciate all your help, Cheryl. The place looks fantastic…'

By ten to seven, Rose was showered and ready. Bagpipe music wafted across the room, from the CD player, and turnips boiled, on the hob. Cheryl and Susie had left about half-an-hour ago. Rose tucked a black curl behind her ear and took two tumblers out of the kitchen cupboard, for the whiskey. It wasn't her usual tipple. In fact she didn't like anything strong. Perhaps she could add water and… A bleep from her phone interrupted her thoughts. She read the text. It was from Alistair.

Gus has given me spare ticket to see band in town – hope you don't mind. He didn't want to go alone. See you tomorrow. Don't eat all those leftovers by yourself!

Rose's bottom lip gave a small wobble as she put her phone on the kitchen table. What a fool she'd been - fancy going to all this trouble, without making her invitation to Alistair sound more formal. An ache swelled in her chest. All jokes aside, the evening would have been her way of saying that, actually, Alistair's friendship meant a lot. He'd helped her through those challenging first months of living away from her parents. He was handy, too, having fixed her hair-dryer and twice unblocked the kitchen sink. She'd so been looking forward to cheering him up, when he was missing the Burns Night celebration back in Scotland.

With heavy steps, she made her way over to the hob and stared at the haggis. The man in the deli had said to simmer it for three hours. It wouldn't be ready until eight o'clock. Rose took a deep breath and tried to think of someone else she could invite over to share it with her. Except that it all seemed kind of silly now. In any case, a lot of her new friends were vegetarian. At least that was one thing she and Alistair had in common – they both loved sausages and burgers. Plus mint toffees were their favourites and they'd got through a whole bagful recently, on a cinema trip. With a sigh, Rose went through to the lounge and sat on the tatty sofa. She picked up a magazine and flicked through, without really reading a word. Suddenly the doorbell rang. She looked at her watch – it was half-past seven. Rose opened the front door.

'Alistair? What are you doing here? I thought you couldn't make it.'

He shuffled his feet. 'Och, Gus found someone else to go with and…'

'Liar!'

He cleared his throat and sighed. 'How come you always know when I'm bending the truth?'

'Dunno. Probably just because we spend a lot of time together. So… What really happened?'

'I just fancied some good old home-cooking instead of a noisy night out…'

Rose raised one eyebrow and folded her arms.

'It's true!' he said with a sheepish smile. 'But, well, okay - I also bumped into your housemates. They, um, weren't impressed when I explained my change of plan for this evening. In fact, they got quite cross, so I figured *you* must have been bending the truth about just cooking up leftovers.'

Rose's cheeks felt hot.

'And Gus did manage to find someone else to ask, after all.' He stared at her for a moment. 'Is that a scarf, around your waist?'

'Um, yes – it must look bonkers.'

Alistair grinned. 'Not particularly. I'm used to your sense of fashion, by now. So… Can I come in?'

Rose stood back, to let him pass, now wondering if the bagpipe music was a bit over the top. Alistair sniffed and went over to the stove. He turned around to look at Rose.

'Haggis? Neeps? What's going on?'

'I, um, know you're missing home, so-'

'What's that music?' he said and went into the lounge. He bent over to the coffee table and read the front page of a sheaf of papers. 'Robbie Burns' poems?'

'I printed them out for us to read, later on,' said Rose, who'd followed him, cheeks even hotter than before. 'I'm sorry Cheryl and Susie gave you a hard time.'

'They didn't have to do much, to persuade me to come,' he said. 'As soon as they hinted that you'd something special planned, I just pictured your disappointed face and…'

'And what?'

'My stomach twisted,' he said, softly, and took her hands. 'I'm not joking – physically, it hurt.'

Rose's voice wavered. 'I felt like that, when I got your text. It's silly, I don't know why…'

'Don't you?' he said softly, and squeezed her fingers.

They looked at each other and Rose's heart raced. All of a sudden her feelings became clear.

'There's a famous Robbie Burns song, you know, called "*A Red, Red, Rose*",' he murmured, in his adorable accent. 'It's all about a bonny lass and could have been written about you.' Alistair leant forward and kissed her on the cheek. When he drew back, her eyes shone. 'I've wanted to do that for such a long time, Rose, but wasn't sure you felt the same…'

Her stomach tingled. Cheryl and Susie would be thrilled that they'd been right, all along.

'We *can't* get together,' she whispered. 'My housemates will never let me live it down!'

They smiled at each other as bagpipe music played on, in the background.

'I've a feeling this is going to be the best Burns Night, ever,' said Alistair. 'So, thank you, my wee Sassenach.'

'What exactly does that mean?' she said and reached up, to wrap her arms around his neck.

'Och, Scots use it as an, um, *affectionate* term for you Saxon English,' he said, innocently.

'Affectionate? Why do I get the feeling that really is bending the truth,' she said and chuckled.

Alistair grinned, before kissing her on the lips. He may not have spent the evening in his beloved Scotland, but for the first time in ages, he felt like he was home.

6
ICING ON THE CAKE

Trevor smoothed down his tie and undid his jacket buttons. It was half-past two. He sat on the terracotta sofa. They had thirty minutes to drive to their daughter's house, to take part in... He shook his head... A *gender-reveal* party.

'Are you almost ready, love?' he hollered.

'No need to shout,' said Angela and smiled as she walked into the lounge.

'You look beautiful, Ang. I've always liked that green dress.'

'Thanks, darling. You don't look so bad yourself.' She glanced at her watch. 'Shall we leave in ten minutes? I just rang Deborah - she's running a bit late. We don't want to get there too early in case she's busy with last minute preparations. I offered to help, but...'

They grinned at each other. Deborah had always been fiercely independent. Perhaps that would change later this year, when she gave birth to her first child.

'Explain this party to me once again,' said Trevor and his brow furrowed.

Angela sat down next to him. 'You know Deborah went for a scan at the hospital, last week?'

He nodded.

'Well, she and Tom asked the radiographer to write down the sex of the baby on a piece of paper and seal it in an envelope. They handed this to a cake-maker who read it privately and as a result has made an, um, appropriate cake.'

'So, when they slice it today, it'll either be pink or blue sponge inside?' said Trevor and ran a hand through his grey-streaked hair.

'Yes. Apparently this sort of celebration is the latest craze from America.'

'Doesn't surprise me,' muttered Trevor.

Playfully, Angela thumped his arm. 'It's not like you to be set in your ways.'

'I'm not!' he said. 'It just seems strange – announcing something as important as that, in public.'

'Well, it is only in front of her family and close friends.' Angela glanced sideways at her husband. 'Anyway, you're a fine one to question breaking boundaries. What about our wedding cake? You persuaded me to have an ultra-modern, chocolate one.'

Trevor sat back into the sofa and chuckled. 'Well, it was the Eighties. Remember my Auntie Barbara's face? She was horrified we'd chosen a large, one-tiered sponge, instead of a tall, fruit cake.'

Angela nodded. 'Remember how she explained it was tradition to have several layers piled high? How in mediaeval times, the couple would kiss over the top and if the cake didn't topple over, it was a sign of a prosperous marriage?'

'Yes. And didn't the white icing represent purity and wealth? Well, we didn't have two pennies to rub together, anyway – not even enough for a honeymoon. Auntie Barbara said the fruit was important as it represented fertility. Yet chocolate chips did for us – you were pregnant the next year.'

'Not everyone was disappointed with it,' said Angela. 'My gran loved chocolate; said rich fruit cake always gave her indigestion. I took the leftover slices to the next church committee meeting and everyone agreed it made a pleasant change from the usual stodgy wedding cake.'

'Deborah's christening cake was another matter for contention,' said Trevor. 'Or rather *cakes*. Remember Jean, from over the road?'

'Yes. She couldn't believe we'd chosen a selection of baby-themed pink-iced cupcakes instead of one big sponge.' Angela stared into the distance for a moment. 'I'll never forget Deborah's first birthday party and how excited we were to light that one candle.'

'Then before we knew it, our daughter was making cakes for us.'

'That pyramid-shaped one you helped her bake one Mother's Day was quite wonderful,' said Angela. 'She was eleven and had just been studying the Ancient Egyptians.'

'I hardly did anything, apart from supervise the use of the oven.' He smiled. 'Even back then, she liked to achieve things by herself.'

'Hmm, I only recall you making a cake once,' said Angela and giggled. 'It was when I had morning sickness. Someone told you ginger would help. I really appreciated all the effort you went to - even if your ginger cake didn't rise and, erm, looked more like an oblong biscuit.'

'Well, what about the gluten-free cake you baked for the first time we met Tom,' said Trevor, a twinkle in his eyes. 'It wasn't up to your usual high standards.'

Angela groaned. 'I'd never heard of Coeliac's disease before and it was the first time I'd used gluten-free flour. Remember how gloopy it went in the middle? Tom, bless him, insisted on eating a second slice and taking home what was left.'

'That was a brilliant gluten-free cake he made for my Fiftieth last year,' said Trevor. 'I suppose he's always had to bake for himself and knows which are the best ingredients.' He consulted his watch. 'Come on, love. We'd better get going. I'm still not convinced about this party, but if it's important to Deborah and Tom, I wouldn't want to be a minute late. I'll fetch the camera.'

They both stood up and Angela slipped her arms around his waist. 'It'll be a lovely afternoon,' she said. 'I still can't believe our little girl is about to become a mum.'

'And we're about to become grandparents.'

She kissed him on the lips, before they headed for the hall. Then, camera and bottle of champagne in a carrier bag, smart shoes on, they went out into the autumn sunshine and got into the car.

Half-an-hour later, they were sitting on another sofa, made from black leather, in Deborah and Tom's lounge. The final guests had just arrived. Deborah and Tom stood in the middle of the room, by a glass coffee table.

Stomach fluttering, Angela gazed around. She winked at her own mother, and nodded at Trevor's parents. Deborah and Tom's best friends sat on the carpet, with their toddler twins. Auntie Barbara stood by the fireplace and a chuckle rising in her chest, Angela wondered what she thought to the whole gender-reveal idea. Tom's mum and dad sat next to their other son on dining room chairs that had been brought into the lounge.

'Thanks so much for coming, everyone,' said Deborah. 'We're really pleased you're all here to witness this special event.'

'This baby means the world to us,' said Tom, 'regardless of its gender. As long as it's healthy, we'll be over the moon, either way. Yet whilst finding out whether it's a boy or a girl, isn't the main thing for us, it's still very exciting - and to share that moment with the people we care for most is really...' he smiled. '... the icing on the cake.'

A lump in her throat, Angela squeezed Trevor's hand. He gave a smile and lifted the camera up to his face. With bated breath, everyone watched as Tom and Deborah knelt on the floor. They cut into a cake, positioned in the centre of the coffee table on a large plate. Delicate swirls of yellow decorated the white icing. On the top lay a marzipan baby and moses basket.

'Here we go!' said Deborah, as they made another cut and pulled out a slice.

Gasps filled the room, just as Trevor's camera clicked.

'It's a boy!' announced Tom, as everyone stared at the blue sponge.

Deborah's eyes filled with tears. Angela and Tom's mother exchanged wide smiles. Even Auntie Barbara had to blow her nose. Trevor put down the camera, stood up and raised his glass.

'Here's to Deborah and Tom,' he said, voice wavering, 'and their son.'

After a sip of champagne, excited chatter filled the room. Angela insisted on helping Deborah hand around sandwiches and fill up drinks, whilst Trevor and Tom's dad jokingly argued about which football team the new baby should support. Unexpectedly, Auntie Barbara thought the cake was a splendid idea and couldn't wait to tell her friends.

'Enjoying yourself?' said Angela later on, when she and Trevor had a moment together.

'You were right, Ang.' He cleared his throat. 'It's been

a great day. Seeing Deborah's face when she saw the colour of the sponge, it... it's something I'll not forget. Guess it's been a wake-up call to me, not to become a stick in the mud. In fact, I'm now inspired to practise my baking skills and come up with some really original cake, for your Fiftieth next spring. Tom's said he'll help and his mum's going to email me some recipes after Christmas.'

'I'm a very lucky lady,' said Angela, softly. 'Auntie Barbara might have worried we'd jinxed our marriage by not kissing over tall tiers of white-iced fruit, but I'm still as happy as the day we said our vows in church.' She squeezed his arm. 'You're definitely the icing on my cake, Trevor Hamilton.'

7
CHERRY BLOSSOM FOR CONFETTI

Pete grinned. 'You know my Jules. She'd never allow guests to throw something that wasn't biodegradable. Her best mate, Lydia, has a flowering tree in her garden and will collect a boxful of petals just before she leaves for the church.'

'What about rice?'

'Sensible as she is, my Jules is a woman, remember. Confetti – it's pretty. Despite her protestations, she must have a secret hankering for pink.'

Both men smiled.

'Well, make the most of tonight, my friend,' said Andy and raised his beer. 'After Saturday, Jules will be cracking the whip. Any last minute nerves?'

'Nope,' said Pete, a bit too quickly, and flipped a beer mat on the mahogany table. 'I'm marrying the woman of my dreams.' Indeed, the last five years with Julie had been the best of his life. But now that the Big Day was approaching, he had wondered if getting married would change everything.

'What's this crazy idea about a tandem bike?' Andy took off his leather jacket. 'There's no fancy wedding motor?'

'Jules' cousin is driving us to and from church in his electric car, but we'll start our cycling honeymoon around Northern France straight after the reception. When you all wave us off, we'll be on a tandem bike, rucksacks on our back. It'll only take us an hour to get to the train station.'

'And let me guess – the wedding breakfast is vegetarian.' Andy clapped Pete on the back. 'If you ever have kids, they'll never get to see inside of a McDonalds. It'll be tofu instead of turkey for Christmas.'

Pete took a swig of his lager. Andy was a good mate, but not the most tactful bloke in the world. Yet he had a point. Jules had already talked about organic baby food and using washable, non-disposable nappies and when their little niece came to stay, Jules was much stricter than him about baths and bed times. What if they didn't agree on stuff like that? He offered Andy a handful of peanuts.

'What about you and Megan tying the knot?' A wicked smile crossed Pete's face.

Andy almost choked. 'Please. Don't make jokes like that, Petey Boy. You know she's been driving me mad, of late.' He shrugged. 'As it happens, we split up last night. I just couldn't take it anymore. At last I've got my independence back.'

Pete raised his eyebrows.

'Take my favourite hobby,' said Andy. 'She started timing me – *allowing* me one hour playing my video games each night. *One hour*? It's my way of relaxing after a hard day in the office. She never understood that.'

Pete's fiancée wouldn't dream of setting a stopwatch, not that his love of TV games was obsessive. In fact sometimes Jules would fetch him a coke, join him on the sofa with a novel and giggle every time he groaned at a poor score.

'As for the soppy movies,' continued Andy. 'If she wanted us to watch one together, I'd agree and sit through it for Brownie points. Then the next day I'd call in the favour and insist on chilling out, in front of the football.'

'A kind of tit for tat system?' said Pete. He flicked the beer mat again. Thank goodness he and Jules didn't work that way. She had her volunteer work, and he had the gym. Busy as life was, they made sure to set special nights aside to eat dinner together. Jules would even buy him a steak from the butchers, as long as it came from humanely reared stock. She never suggested he helped her with charity work, although last Christmas he'd gone along to the homeless soup kitchens with her, and quite enjoyed himself. Nor did he try to convince her to lift weights, when on January the First she'd patted her thighs and said this was the year to get fit. Between them they'd decided to take up a new sport together and went swimming at the local pool, once a week.

'Nah. I'm well out of it,' said Andy and drained his pint. 'Freedom again. I can come and go as I choose. Live off takeaway. Be in charge of the remote control.'

Pete got up to buy the next round. Jules was a great cook, whereas they both agreed his strength was the washing up. As for the remote control, Jules had a mean trick of getting it by tickling him under the armpits until he begged her to stop.

Whilst waiting to order the drinks, Pete smiled to himself, took out his mobile from his jeans pocket and dialled his favourite number.

'Hello gorgeous,' he said quietly into the phone, his stomach tingling. 'Just leaving a message to say you really are the best.'

Jules replied via text. 'Did he know that Andy had proposed to Megan last night, but she'd turned him down, saying that she wasn't ready to settle down yet?'

Pete glanced over towards his friend. His eyes scoured

the receding hairline, flash leather coat and slightly too wide grin. Pete shook his head. Poor Andy wasn't the most tactful bloke in the world, yet could never be honest about the things that mattered.

He texted back to Jules: "I'll take him for a curry later – try to get him to open up, over his favourite dish.'

'Okay. Love you,' she replied.

'Love you, too,' typed Pete. 'Can't wait to kiss my missus under showers of Cherry Blossom confetti."

8

MIDSUMMER KNIGHT'S DREAM

'Handsome Prince Philip from "Sleeping Beauty" was my favourite,' said Mel and with a spoon scooped up her last mouthful of cereal.

Grace yawned. 'Cheeky Peter Pan was mine - although Robin Hood was very daring. Then there was determined Pongo from 101 Dalmations…'

Mel snorted. 'They're all a bit quirky – what about Prince Charming from Snow White? Or muscle-bound Tarzan? Now they really *were* heroes.' She grinned. 'We certainly watched a lot of films when we were little. Remember how Gran often used to sit with us and knit at the same time?'

'Happy Days,' said Grace and tightened the belt of her dressing gown, before filling the kettle.

'I can't understand why you haven't had a date for so long, sis… You clearly aren't too fussy, when it comes to heroes,' Mel teased. 'I mean, Pongo was a dog, for goodness sake!'

Grace shrugged. Her sister had a point. It was almost one year since she'd been on more than a first date. After studying, away, to be a teacher, it had been difficult settling back in the village, even though now she wouldn't swap her life here for the world. The two sisters rented a cottage together and after a busy day in the city, it was bliss to leave the hustle and bustle behind, and relax in the rural calm - although Mel often found the energy to go disco-dancing after a long day on her feet. Grace would rather read a good book or pop around to her parents' bungalow for one of Mum's amazing hot chocolates.

'I can't believe you've not met someone at work,' continued Mel. She stood up and smoothed down her navy uniform.

'Working in a primary school isn't like a big hospital, even if they are both in the city. Most of the teachers are women and the only three men are over forty and married.' Grace shrugged again. 'I'm glad I moved back to be near you – and Mum and Dad - but let's face it…'

Mel nodded. 'Here in the village, we know most people inside out.' Her face lit up. 'Of course! I forgot to tell you - my department needs a new scanner, and we're trying to think of fundraising ideas. Jake, the new physiotherapist, suggested a Progressive Dinner and…'

Grace's brow furrowed.

'It's where you move from house to house for each course. According to him, they're a lot of fun, and every diner who isn't cooking pays an agreed sum. People have already offered to host and prepare the starter, main, and cheeseboard… Why don't we do desserts at ours?'

'And how is that going to help me find my Knight in Shining Armour?' said Grace. Not that she really believed in such things.

Mel chuckled. 'Just wait until you meet Jake. He's got the strength of one of those fictional vampires you like, and as for his arm muscles...' She sighed. 'It's a good thing I've got my Alan or you'd have competition.'

'Aren't you two celebrating your two year anniversary sometime soon?'

Mel's eyes shone. 'Yes. Next week. We're going out for

a Chinese meal. Anyway, how about it? Romantic intentions aside, I'm sure the evening will be great. Plus it's all for a good cause.'

Grace rolled her eyes. 'Mel, no offence, but your past attempts at matchmaking haven't been exactly successful. Take that hospital porter you arranged for me to go bowling with...'

'How was I to know that he'd just handed in his notice and was off to do volunteer work in Africa?'

'What about Alan's brother? He spent the whole evening telling me how he used to hate school, especially his teacher in Reception.'

'I think he was nervous.' Mel giggled.

'I'm only twenty-three. We're not in the nineteenth century – there's no rush for me to find someone.'

Mel looked serious for a moment. 'Yes, but sis... It's nice, isn't it, being part of a couple?'

Grace put two slices of bread in the toaster and went to collect the post, which she'd just heard fall through the letter box. Mel was right. Even though Grace didn't live alone, sometimes she felt... out on the edge.

Just as the toast popped up, she came back into the kitchen, holding an opened ivory silk envelope. She mustered a smile.

'What is it?' said Mel.

'An invitation – to Cousin Linda's wedding on the twentieth of August.'

'Ooh, great,' said Mel. 'I wondered when that would get here. That means we've got two months to find outfits. I love a posh summer do.'

Grace passed the card and envelope to Mel and headed to the fridge, for the butter. As a single person, family get-togethers were the most challenging thing, like baby

Lucy's christening, last spring. At least three relatives interrogated Grace about her love-life. She gave a wry smile, as she recalled good old Gran saying, in a loud voice, that her granddaughter had better things to do than chase men and that love would find a way, in its own time.

She sighed and spread jam over the butter. Could this new physiotherapist really be The One? She'd seen how Alan soothed Mel after a hard day at on the ward and missed that closeness. Yet this Jake sounded more like the bulked-up cartoon heroes Mel liked.

Come on, she told herself and cut the slices of toast in half. Whatever happened to a half-full glass? Just because he was more like her sister's type, didn't completely rule out the chance of a spark between him and Grace.

'If we prepare cold desserts in advance, we'll be able to go out and take part in the rest of the dinner,' said Grace. 'It sounds good - are the houses far apart?'

'The starter and main are at locations in the city. Normally it would make sense to stay there for all the courses, but when Shirley...'

'The receptionist on your ward who lives opposite the post office?' said Grace.

Mel nodded. 'When she mentioned that her husband manages a deli and specializes in cheese, well... It was a done deal!'

Grace grinned. 'I suppose that makes us the perfect choice for puddings, then, as we're only about a fifteen minute walk from her house. Then after cheese at hers, everyone will just have the half-an-hour train journey back to the city. Talking of which...' Grace nodded to the clock. 'You'd better get off to work.'

'Just one thing,' said Mel and picked up her light

jacket, from the back of a chair. 'The dinner is this Saturday night and I'm working all day, from very early on. It won't be worth me coming back, in the evening, so I'd meet you at the first house, in the city - it's near the hospital. But I could help cook our desserts on Friday night. Plus we'll need to spruce up the lounge and wash down the garden furniture, in case people want to sit out in the garden.'

'Don't worry.' Grace smiled. 'I know you'll be shattered and it's easy for me, I have the whole of Saturday off. But we'll choose the recipes together.'

Mel beamed, before knocking back her orange juice and heading out to the hallway. After pouring a coffee, Grace heard the front door open and then slam shut. Forty-five minutes later, she stood in the hallway, showered and dressed. Grace opened the door. Dew glistened on the lawn and clouds clustered around the early morning sun, so like her sister, she slipped into a light rain jacket, before leaving for the train station.

As she walked up the drive, a van pulled up outside the house of Dee and Bert, her retired neighbours. A young man, about her own age, in jeans and a checked shirt got out, fawn curly hair waving in the wind. In the passenger seat of his van, a golden retriever sat serenely, like a royal on tour.

'Morning, Grace!' called a sing-song voice. It was Dee, in her dressing gown, striding towards the young man.

Grace walked along the pavement to meet her neighbour.

Dee straightened her gold-rimmed glasses. 'Goodness, dear, this is an early start for me! I'd like you to meet my nephew, Sam.'

'Hi,' he said. Grace noticed a leather bracelet, around

his wrist, as he gently shook her hand.

What lovely caramel eyes, she thought. They reminded Grace of her favourite chocolate bar. And was that a stud earring? Her stomach tingled. Quirky, he was, indeed.

'Have you come far?' she asked, thinking how well-behaved the dog was, not even barking to be let out of the van.

'Only about half a mile.' Those caramel eyes twinkled.

'Sam's moved into the terraced house that was up for rent in Oak Meadow Avenue,' said Dee. 'Now that his mum's...'

'Oh, of course... I'm so sorry for your loss...' stuttered Grace. She remembered just in time that Dee's sister had passed away, several months ago. Apparently Sam's dad left his mum shortly after he was born.

'Sam's working for Mr Brooks, who owns the hardware shop,' said Dee. 'As soon as I saw the advert for that position, I knew it would be perfect for my nephew. He'd just lost his job as a handyman and well...' Her eyes crinkled. 'It made sense and I'm thrilled to have him living so near.'

'So, if you ever need anything fixing, Grace, just let me know,' Sam said and winked. Her stomach tingled again and suddenly she wished her tumble dryer or boiler had packed up.

'I always loved visiting Auntie Dee as a child, so it's a wish come true to move here,' he said. 'It's the perfect place to settle and have children, don't you think?'

Grace nodded. He was a family man, as well!

'However, I won't be living the good life if I'm late for work and get sacked,' Sam continued. 'So, auntie, this is just a quick visit to...'

Grace smiled, made her excuses and turned around. As

she walked back along the pavement, the breeze carried Sam's words. Bless, he'd invited his aunt and uncle to dinner to see what he'd done with the place. But then he muttered something about a "Holly" being a bit off colour, so he'd cook them all something plain, like chicken and rice…'

Grace's heart sank. Typical – the first interesting man to cross her path in months and he'd obviously already got a girlfriend. No wonder he'd talked about settling down. Perhaps he was already married, and just didn't wear a wedding band. Maybe this Holly was pregnant and had morning sickness.

With a shake, Grace braced herself for the day ahead, teaching thirty nine year-olds, and told herself not to worry – according to Mel she was going to serve dessert to the dream man, at the weekend. She really hoped so. Now the pressure was on to find a date for Linda's wedding, so that she could avoid another uncomfortable interrogation.

***

Butterflies fluttered in Grace's chest, at the prospect of her imminent meeting with Jake, the supposed man of her dreams. She washed up her lunch dishes and stood in front of the cooker. Saturday had dawned warm and cheerful with lawnmowers whirring and goldfinches splashing in the birdbath. Lunch had been more of a mid-afternoon snack, as she'd spent the morning cleaning the lounge and bathroom thoroughly, plus washing the garden furniture. Mel had gone to work bright and early and now was the time for Grace to start preparing desserts. All week Mel had chatted about Jake. Apparently he liked horror movies, just like Grace, plus he read novels and his favourite food was the same as hers - fish.

Perhaps, after all, they were well suited. So, the day before Grace had her hair trimmed and splashed out on a knee-length red dress. Poor Jake. No doubt Mel had spent the last few days subjecting him to twenty questions. She just hoped that her sister had been more subtle than usual, and not laboured the point that Grace was single and keen to date.

At least Mel had found out that one of his favourite desserts was chocolate soufflé, which Grace would make as well as meringue fruit tarts. Well, they did say that the way to a man's heart was through his stomach. She would prepare the soufflé batter in advance, to be popped in the oven, just after they all arrived from eating the main course, in the city.

On Thursday she'd practised, and the soufflés went a little flat in the middle. Therefore she researched on the computer and discovered that for this kind of dessert, getting just the right oven temperature was of maximum importance. Which was why, a while later, she paced the kitchen, stomach knotted. She'd switched the oven on, before making the pastry for the fruit tarts and it wasn't heating up.

'Oh no,' she muttered to herself and wiped her brow. She left it another fifteen minutes, then opened the door. The oven still felt stone cold. At that moment the doorbell rang and she went to answer. A delivery man handed her a package. As she said goodbye to him, out of the corner of her eye she spotted Sam's van, outside Dee's house. Well he had said to let him know if anything needed fixing – and of course she'd pay him for any help.

Hurriedly, she went around to her neighbour and knocked on the door. Dee answered. Sam's golden retriever meandered up to Grace and sniffed her hand.

'Come on, girl,' said Sam and gently pulled the dog away. 'She must like you,' he said, caramel eyes twinkling. 'Normally she growls if I'm in the presence of a strange woman.'

'I hope you mean strange as in unfamiliar, and not odd,' Grace said and laughed.

'Honestly, Sam,' said Dee and shook her head, nevertheless smiling. 'Grace, is everything all right, dear?'

Rambling, Grace explained about the Progressive Dinner and asked if there was any way Sam could pop around, to at least find out what was wrong with the oven. Minutes later, he stood in her kitchen.

'It'll be the thermostat – or element,' he said and fiddled with his leather bracelet. 'I'll have to pull out the cooker and remove its back, to take a look.'

Please let Sam be mistaken, she thought - let the oven start working again, any minute. Otherwise, what kind of dessert could she make? Chocolate mousse was the nearest thing to soufflé, but not nearly as impressive – and not Jake's favourite, either. At this rate she'd never get a date for Linda's wedding!

Then Grace's cheeks flushed. Honestly, it was ridiculous, her trying to make everything perfect for a man she hadn't even met. As for the upcoming nuptials, Grace was a strong woman and shouldn't be fazed by curious questions. In any event, Gran would be there for moral support.

She shook her head. Why, once again, had she gone along with Mel's matchmaking? Perhaps this setback was a reminder that, like Gran would say, love was one of those things that chose its own moment to appear and couldn't be forced.

'It's as I thought,' said Sam, and stood up. 'The element's cracked. You'll need a new one.'

'Thanks,' she said and smiled. 'I really appreciate you taking a look.'

Sam grinned. 'I can do better than that – this is a popular model of cooker. We stock replacement elements at work. I can pop into the shop and pick one up. I get every other Saturday off, and you're in luck, today is one of them. I can nip straight back here and fit it, in time for tonight. It's not a big job.'

'No… I couldn't possibly… I mean…' What would his partner, Holly think? Wouldn't it disrupt their weekend?

Sam chuckled. 'Are you always this indecisive? Honestly, Grace, it's no trouble. You've been a good neighbour to my aunt and uncle. Dee told me how you picked up shopping and prescriptions for them, when they both had flu last winter. One good turn deserves another.'

Grace's chest glowed. 'Well… If you're sure - that would be great. And to prove I don't usually dither so much, how about I insist on having coffee and biscuits ready, for when you get back?' Apart from anything else, Sam mending it would save having to call out a handyman from the phone book.

'Mine's white with two sugars!' said Sam and gave the thumbs up, before taking out his car keys and heading for the hallway.

As good as his word, Dee's nephew was back in thirty minutes, and a couple of hours later, near five o'clock, the oven was fixed. They'd even had time for him to take a break and stroll around her garden. It was a humid day and Grace made them both iced lemonades. He was good company, chatting about his favourite plants and filling the golden summer air with his infectious laugh.

Grace decided it was quicker not to make pastry, so would just provide meringue nests instead of tarts. Now she'd make the soufflé batter, and put it in the fridge until they got back from eating the main course, in the city. They wouldn't take long to bake.

'Thanks, again,' said Grace, when Sam was back in the kitchen, having gone outside to answer his phone. 'I'll get my cheque book – how much do I owe you, for your time?'

'Don't be silly!' he said, and stood in the porch. 'Like I said, one good turn deserves another.'

'At least let me pay you for the element!' She smiled. 'I would invite you to join the Progressive Dinner this evening – my treat – as a thank you, but I guess you need to check on Holly.' Grace blushed. 'Sorry, I couldn't help hearing, the other day, that's she'd been ill.'

Sam's eyes lost their shine for a moment. 'Hmm. I was really worried, but she seems to be picking up.' He thought for a moment. 'Erm what time train are you catching, into the city, for the starter and main?'

'The six thirty. Why?'

Sam looked at his watch. 'That gives me time to check on Holly and change. I'd like to accept your invitation, if that's okay? It'd be great to get to know auntie and uncle's neighbours a little better…' He grinned, 'Seeing as I'm sticking around.'

'Oh… Um…Holly won't mind?'

He shook his head. 'No – that was Dee on the phone, ringing to see how I was doing. Bert's out at a golf do later on. She fancies getting some fresh air herself, tonight, and wondered if Holly was up to accompanying her to the Lake Café. One of her friends from the Woman's Institute will meet them there.'

'It's a lovely evening for sitting out,' said Grace.

He nodded. 'I'd only be in the way – apparently they are going to brain storm ideas for a charity bake-off and making cakes rise isn't my strong point!'

Grace smiled and for some reason her stomach tingled again, even though she knew he was spoken for. 'Okay, but the cheque...'

'Give me it later,' he said, on his way out.

After he'd left, Grace quickly prepared the batter and changed into her new dress. She decided not to wear her new, bright red lipstick. She and Jake would get on if the chemistry was right - fancy cosmetics wouldn't make any difference.

Despite chiding herself for setting her sights on a stranger, just so that she didn't go to a wedding on her own, Grace still made sure she spent time with Jake, seeing as Mel had gone to an effort to match them together. She sat next to him during the starter, whilst at the other end of the table, Sam talked comfortably to Mel and a couple of her nursing colleagues. They seemed smitten with his easy manner. He'd exchanged his gold stud earring for a hoop and wore a different, smart grey and white checked shirt with immaculate dark blue jeans – and cowboy boots! That infectious laugh of his accompanied the butternut soup and made it very hard for Grace to listen to Jake's every word.

What made it even more difficult, however, was that Jake and Grace actually had... not so much in common. Whilst Grace liked romantic horror movies, with well-meaning ghosts or vampires, Jake preferred the really frightening ones. Plus Grace loved novels set in exotic places around the world, whilst Jake read nothing but crime novels with English characters. As for them both liking fish, Jake's favourite was traditional cod and chips or scampi in a basket, whilst Grace loved the more adventurous raw Sushi or lightly grilled Tuna steaks.

So, in any event, Jake didn't turn out to be the man of her dreams - although she had no doubt he'd be perfect, for someone else. He listened politely, laughed at her jokes and his athletic build would impress most women. Jake just didn't make her stomach tingle like... someone else did.

As they all walked twenty minutes to the next house and sat down to the main meal – Beef Wellington with delicious roast potatoes – Sam strolled next to Grace and chatted about his love of travelling far and wide. He'd backpacked around Australia, Iceland and the Far East. Grace told him about a novel she'd just read set in Japan, and how one day she'd love to visit there. As for movies, Sam loved supernatural ones and they had a humorous conversation about whether werewolves could ever really exist.

'Grace!' whispered Mel, who was sitting by her sister, as the main meal came to an end. She jerked her head towards Jake, who was chatting animatedly to one of the other nurses. 'Why aren't you sitting next to him, again? Tonight's your big chance.'

'Sorry, but he's not really my type.' Grace blushed.

'Honestly, there's no helping some people,' said Mel, with mock indignation, her eyes nevertheless twinkling.

Grace smiled and turned back to Sam who was reading a text on his phone. His brow furrowed, the caramel eyes dull for a second.

'Everything okay?' she said.

He shook his head. 'Holly's not one hundred percent

again. It's nothing serious, but...' Sam smiled sheepishly.

'I understand,' said Grace, stomach twisting. 'You want to be with her.'

'Yep - sorry – I've got to go. But I've enjoyed tonight.'

'Look, let me come back with you on the train,' said Grace, noticing how his shoulders sagged. 'It'll give me chance to open up the house, get the lights on and drinks ready and batter out of the fridge...'

'Are you sure?' he said.

'Definitely.' Briefly she explained to Mel and then followed Sam outside and towards the train station.

'By the way,' said Sam as they sat down in the train. 'You, erm, look great. That dress really suits your blonde hair.'

She blushed.

'Holly always suits that colour. I won't buy her a collar unless it's red.'

'*Collar*?' Grace's eyebrows shot into her forehead.

'Yep – she is micro-chipped, but still, I'd never let her off the lead, without some obvious I.D. on.'

'Holly's a dog?' Of course - the golden retriever.

'Erm, yes...' Sam chuckled. 'Why? Who did you think she was?'

'Oh, um, well...' She cleared her throat. 'I assumed she was human, when I heard you saying to Dee that you'd cook chicken and rice for everyone...'

'And I did,' he said grinning. 'I just added some spices and herbs to the platefuls for us humans. It's a very good meal for a sickly dog. Holly's been out of sorts all week, but the vet says it's nothing much to worry about.'

'Oh – now I feel stupid,' Grace muttered, but couldn't help laughing with Sam and her heart almost skipped a beat.

'Believe me, if Holly wasn't ill she'd have jumped up and barked when you called around today.'

'She must mean an awful lot to you.'

He bit his lip. 'Yes, Mum gave her to me, four years ago, the Christmas after she was diagnosed... She's made the move much easier here – I'd have rattled around in a cottage, on my own.'

So, there was no wife or partner. Holly the dog was his only companion. Poor Sam must have been so worried when she fell ill. Grace squeezed his arm.

'Why don't you and Holly come around for lunch tomorrow?' she said. 'I could do chicken and rice, followed by a nice walk in the park – if Holly's improved. There might even be some chocolate soufflés left over, for the two-legged ones amongst us.'

Sam smiled. 'I'd like that a lot. Thanks, Grace.'

'I'll get your cheque ready, as well – to pay for the element,' she said. 'You really saved the day. To whom do I make it payable?'

'Sam Knight,' he said.

A surge of warmth spread through Grace's chest. It looked like Knights in Shining Armour – or at least checked shirts - did exist.

9

SWEET TALK

'No whistling this morning, love?' said Craig as Moira slipped on a lightweight jacket and picked up her handbag. 'You've been quiet ever since you got in from work yesterday. I thought you were tired.' Craig put down his briefcase. 'Anything the matter?'

'It's nothing really.' Moira smiled brightly. 'Go on, you hurry up. The village dentist can't be late.'

'I've worked hard all these years to be my own boss.' He smiled back. 'I think I deserve a couple of minutes. In any case, my first appointment isn't until ten.'

'Okay. It's just...' Moira shrugged. 'I'm being silly, but ever since Ross left home for university last autumn, I've been wondering, now that I've got more time, should I take on a more demanding job. The money would come in useful.'

'But we manage - and you love working at *Sweet Talk*.' Craig led Moira into the lounge and they sat down on the floral sofa. 'What's brought this on?'

'Remember Ross's new best friend when we first moved here, Andrew? His family left for the city not long after Ross started High school?'

Craig nodded.

'His mam, Alison, paid a fleeting visit to the village yesterday and popped in for a bag of bonbons, favourites of her great-aunt who's just turned eighty.'

Craig's brow furrowed.

'Mrs Hamilton who lives in Hollyhock Cottage,' said Moira.

'Ah yes. Lovely lady. Always brings me a jar of homemade chutney when she calls in for her half-yearly check-up.'

Moira grinned. 'She often mutters how I'm keeping you in business.'

'Not that again.' Craig rolled his eyes and chuckled. It had been a standing joke in the village for years, that Moira tempted the locals with all manner of confectionary, just to ensure Craig's practice thrived.

'Alison has set herself up as a virtual secretary,' said Moira and fiddled with her house keys. 'Apparently they're all the rage these days. You work from home and everything is done on line – you never even meet your clients. She remembered that I'd worked as a secretary before I fell pregnant and said I could easily brush up my skills, if I took an evening course. According to her, this virtual office role can be quite lucrative, as well as challenging.'

'But you'd miss chatting with everyone from the shop,' exclaimed Craig. 'And Ross would never forgive you!'

Moira laughed. They'd moved to the village when Ross had just left Juniors. Having mortgaged themselves to the hilt, Craig had taken over the little dental practice. Eventually she landed a job in *Sweet Talk*. Ross settled easily into the high school, especially when his class-mates found out where Moira worked.

'You have the best job ever, Mam,' Ross used to say. 'One day I'm going to open the coolest sweet shop in Scotland.'

It was funny how things turned out, thought Moira.

Ross used to love helping out in the holidays, replenishing the jars, tidying the pick n' mix bags and cleaning the scoops. Her boss, Chrissie, gave him a paid Saturday job as soon as he turned sixteen and he met many a girlfriend in the Jellybean aisle. Yet now he was training to be a vet and was admirably health conscious, which meant handfuls of nuts instead of Liquorice Allsorts. Although he still dropped into the shop occasionally when he was home, to try out any new flavoured boiled sweets or sherbets.

Moira stood up. 'I'd better get going. We've a delivery of cough pastilles and mints first thing. Chrissie isn't in until lunchtime. She's visiting her granddaughter.' Moira smiled. 'The wee lass will soon be six months old and Chrissie is absolutely smitten.'

Craig kissed his wife on the cheek, before they hurried into the hall and out into the spring sunshine. 'You know I'll support you whatever you decide,' he said and she kissed him back. Hand in hand, they walked past the border of daffodils and towards the high street...

'Goodness, I need a cup of tea,' said Moira to herself, a couple of hours later, after she'd taken the delivery and rearranged all the pastilles, menthol sweets and mint-flavoured humbugs. A small bell rang as the door opened and Mrs McKeith puffed her way in. She'd tied her white-whiskered terrier up outside and closed the door, before leaning on her stick.

'You're just in time, Jean,' said Moira, and pulled out a little wooden stool. Mrs McKeith shuffled over and eased herself down.

'You're a good lass,' she said, in between breaths.

'Tea or coffee, today?'

The old lady's eyes twinkled. 'Whatever you're

having.'

'And then a quarter of your usual Pear Drops, I expect,' called Moira from the kitchenette. Minutes later she returned with two mugs.

Mrs McKeith gazed around the shop. 'I'll never forget when sweet-rationing ended, some years after the war. Us children all emptied our piggy banks. Even our mams were excited when the butcher handed out free chocolate to every customer.' She let her stick fall to the ground.

'How is your leg?' asked Moira.

'Och, I shouldn't grumble. The warmer weather helps. Isn't it a lovely day?'

It certainly was, thought Moira, when, that afternoon she sat on the shop's doorstep, finishing her egg and cress sandwich. Chrissie was inside, chatting to the vicar, no doubt as she weighed out his favourite peppermint creams. The sun warmed Moira's cheeks as she gazed around the village. The post office morning rush was over, but the grocer's was still bustling. She waved to her friend Rose, who rode past on a horse. Moira hadn't been to the stables in ages and with the fresh grassy smells of spring and blue sky, she suddenly longed to go on a hack.

'This is a late lunch,' said Alistair, and grinned as he helped Moira to her feet and they went inside. He'd walked around from the antiques shop next door. 'Haven't treated myself to some peanut brittle for a while,' he said. 'Thought I'd celebrate.'

'Made a good sale, then?' Moira asked and poured tan coloured chunks onto the scales, nodding at the vicar as he left.

'Ay, indeed,' said Alistair and rubbed his hands together. 'Someone had heard about the collection of Japanese egg cups I'd acquired and bought the whole lot.'

'Cake for tea, then.' Moira grinned.

Alistair took out his wallet. 'I thought I'd try out that recipe you gave me for carrot cake. I'm feeling a wee bit more adventurous, now that I've mastered Victoria Sponge.' As Alistair said himself, he was a traditional man and hadn't even known how to scramble eggs for the children's tea. He'd wanted to surprise his wife – Moira's friend Eve - with a cake for her birthday last month and was so proud when his sponge actually rose and tasted good. The couple weren't doing so well, thought Moira, since the recession had forced Eve to commute every day to a new job in a nearby town and they'd both had to take on new roles. People didn't have enough money for old ornaments at the moment - not when they couldn't afford new clothes or shoes.

She handed him the bag of Peanut Brittle and rummaged for another one from under the counter, containing a random collection of boiled sweets. 'Take those for the kids,' she said. 'They're almost out of date or broken. We'd only throw them out.' She smiled. 'Just don't let Eve eat all of them!'

'Really? You're… very kind.' Alistair gave her a wide smile and then humming, left the shop. Chrissie had been watching from the kitchenette door.

'You're great with the customers, Moira,' she said. 'It was a lucky day when I took you on.'

Moira blushed. Craig was right. She loved working here.

'In fact, I was wondering…' Chrissie cleared her throat. 'I'd really like to take a back seat and spend more time with my granddaughter, especially now her mam is going back to work. Would you be interested in managing the shop full-time? It would mean a pay-rise and more of a say in how things are run. I'd be interested in any ideas you've got to boost business… Making *Sweet Talk* more of a success would mean a slice of the profits for you.'

'Really? I mean… Gosh.' Moira beamed. Every so often she'd dreamed of what changes she'd make if this were her shop. 'Thanks, Chrissie… I'd love to. In fact I've already got some ideas. There's an online course I once found, on how to make your own quality fudge and chocolates. We could ask Mr Johnson, from Johnson's Builders, to give the counter under the till a glass front and we'd display them there…'

'And what did she say to that?' asked Craig, as he and Moira ate dinner that night.

'She thought it was wonderful and couldn't understand why she hadn't thought of it herself.'

'You never fail to surprise me,' said Craig. 'I think sales will rocket, once you're selling home-made chocolate. Well done, clever clogs.'

'Hey, enough with the sweet talk.' Moira blushed and gazed out of the patio doors, at the pink and lilac Azaleas. Mind racing, she brainstormed flavours for her home-made chocolates. Perhaps it would be wise to search out a recipe for, say, low-sugar tablet. The last thing she wanted was new rumours spreading across the village, that her venture was nothing but a ploy to keep her dear, dentist husband in business.

10
MESSY BUCKETS

Butterflies in his stomach, Stan boarded his usual section of the morning train, loosened his collar and scanned the carriage. There she was – bobbed, silver-streaked hair straight and slick, knee-length skirt and jacket perfectly pressed. With her tidily rolled-up umbrella and manicured nails, she was sophisticated, elegant and no doubt out of his league.

Yet there was something about her lopsided smile; something about the way she bit her lip when concentrating on one of her magazines. She'd brightened up his morning journey every day for the last week and this would be the final time he saw her until after the weekend.

She caught his eye and gave him one of her smiles before going back to reading. Her magazines were always glossy and covered with photos of famous people he didn't know, but then, like her, they were French. Inwardly he sighed. How had five days passed so quickly, without him daring to say so much as "hello"?

'Why don't you try learning a bit of that woman's language, Dad,' said his daughter, Janet, before tucking into the Sunday roast she'd just prepared. Even though it was the height of summer, and a barbecue might have been more appropriate, she knew how much Stan missed his wife's stuffing and Yorkshire puds. Janet's Mum had died almost four years ago.

'Which woman?' he asked, innocently, in between mouthfuls of beef and potato.

'The one on the train you've been talking about for the last ten minutes.' Janet's eyes twinkled as she passed him the gravy. 'She might appreciate someone making the effort.'

'You think so?' Stan put down his knife and fork, for a moment.

Janet smiled. 'Why not, Dad? Having someone to chat with would certainly make next week's journeys less boring.'

His daughter was right. Then and there Stan decided that the next day, Monday, he'd pluck up the courage to start a conversation. His granddaughter agreed to coach his accent that very afternoon. Quite the expert, she was, due to her studying GCSE French.

When Stan returned to his bungalow that evening, he stood in front of the mirror and practised some more. It seemed so easy, talking to his reflection, but he was no Sacha Distel, with his receding hairline and lack of tan. What if he lost his nerve and ended up speechless? That wouldn't impress classy Marie. It was a nice name, Marie, printed clearly on her rectangular name badge.

Stan assumed she worked somewhere international, like the airport, which was only a few train stops on from his. Sometimes Marie ate a croissant on her journey, before spending ages reading the packaging with foreign writing on it. No doubt French women were health conscious and she was studying the nutritional values. She must have found a local shop that imported her favourite brands of foods.

On Monday morning, Stan got up early and took extra

care shaving and polishing his shoes. His friend, John, joined him at the platform. Right on time, the train pulled in and they boarded.

'How come the weekend goes so quickly?' said John. 'Did you watch the football, Saturday afternoon?'

Stan nodded. 'Good match. Pity we lost at the last minute.'

'Lost? We were robbed of that goal.' John tucked his paper under his arm. 'That's a sharp tie you've got on.'

Stan's cheeks felt hot. He'd bought it especially. It was blue with fine silver stripes. He wanted to make a good impression on Marie who always looked immaculate. A seat became available and Stan insisted John take it. He was happy to stand as, on his feet, he could just about spot Marie, further down the carriage.

As the train approached the next station, John stood up. He and Stan only travelled one stop together. The doors slid open and after saying goodbye, John got off. Stan waved goodbye to him before gazing once more along the rows of seats. Now the space next to Marie was available.

He took a deep breath and heart racing, hurried past the other passengers. As the train pulled away, he sat down beside her.

'Oops. Sorry,' he said, as his briefcase knocked against her leg and yawned open. A pen rolled out onto the floor and she picked it up.

'Merci beaucoup,' he said and took it from her. 'Or, as we used to say back in the day, at school, "Messy buckets".'

He put the briefcase on his lap and looked out of the window. Did he really just say *Messy buckets*? Marie must think him an idiot. However, a few minutes later, cheeks back to their normal colour, undeterred Stan took a deep breath. 'Do you work at the airport?'

Marie shook her head.

His mouth went dry. Perhaps she didn't understand? Okay. Better ask that question in a different way. Stan screwed up his eyes and tried to remember one of the phrases his granddaughter had taught him: 'Travaillez-vous à l'aéroport?'

Marie's eyes crinkled at the corners. 'Why are you talking in French?'

Stan's jaw dropped. 'Your English is really good.'

'Thank you. It's only taken me fifty-one years to perfect.'

'Fifty-one years… You mean…?'

Marie chuckled.

'You're not French,' said Stan, slowly. 'But the magazines… Those croissants with the fancy foreign packaging…' Now he was rambling. She must have thought him very strange to have noticed all those details about her.

'I'm taking a course at evening school,' she said. 'I've just started working at a travel agents and speaking another language would be an asset. I was lucky to get the job, what with all the younger competition – I want to prove that I'm open-minded, about learning new things. As for these…' She lifted up her glossy magazine. 'A large newsagent next to the office sells them. They're not my usual type of reading, but I thought it would do me good to flick through, even though I don't understand much. Same with the croissants - I try to translate the ingredients.' Her mouth twitched. 'Sorry to disappoint.'

'No, not at all, it's just you looked so chic and…'

'What me?' Marie smiled. 'I have to look as neat as a

pin for my job. Normally, I put comfort above appearance and like nothing more than a pair of slacks and T-shirt. At the weekends I don't even straighten my hair.'

'Me neither. Not the hair, I mean, the suit, you see...' He opened his case. She peered in at a pair of folded-up overalls.

'I don't understand.' Marie's brow furrowed.

'I'm a mechanic.'

'So why bother with the smart jacket and trousers?'

'I'm doing jury service for two weeks. Some days it finishes early, so I promised my boss I'd drop into work straight afterwards as they've got a lot of jobs on at the moment. The garage is only a short walk from where I get on the train in the mornings. I've only been there six months after being made redundant and, well... It does no harm to appear keen.'

He rummaged around in his briefcase, delving between a notebook, pens and tissues. Eventually he pulled out a tube of extra strong mints and offered one to Marie. She opened her handbag and searched amongst the spare tights and array of make-up, only to pull out an exact same packet. They smiled at each other.

'If you like,' said Stan, voice firmer now, 'I could bring some chocolate tomorrow. My granddaughter bought it for my birthday. I think it's French. We could share it whilst you examine the ingredients.' He smiled. 'My name's Stan, by the way.'

'That's a great idea, Stan. Very thoughtful. Thank you.' Marie beamed back at him. 'Or should I say, "Messy buckets?"'

11

CHANGING SEASONS

'How can I have been so stupid?' muttered Ruth. Her shoulders sagged as she stared into the empty boot of her car. Her daughter, Ellie, hovered by her side. They had just got to the park, straight from school. It was the end of term and Ruth had carefully planned the picnic trip. Normally it was Gavin who picked Ellie up on the final afternoon of the school year. For that day, it had become something of a tradition for him to arrange a special surprise.

'What's the matter, Mum?' Ellie pulled down her sunhat.

'I've forgotten everything - even my handbag.' Her mind had been all over the place after rushing home from work, as Ruth had navigated her way around cardboard boxes in the hallway. She'd almost tripped over golf clubs belonging to her brother, Ben, before realizing that she was late for the school run. The well-stocked hamper would still be sitting on the kitchen table.

Ruth sighed, shut the boot and gave a wry smile. Was this what it was going to be like, now that she faced life as a single mum, without even Ben around? It had only been a few days, since her brother had gone, and already she'd messed up. It was the beginning of the summer holidays - and the start of a new chapter. Tomorrow she was moving the last of his possessions into storage.

'I'd even bought some of those mini Cornish pasties and toffee cookies you like,' said Ruth. She'd been intent on beginning to make up, in some small way, for this year, so far; to prove that *Mum could cope* and life would still be full of laughter and treats – despite the absence of Ellie's Dad, Ruth's dear husband, Gavin.

Having lived with them for six months, Ruth's brother, Ben, had finally accepted a much longed-for promotion, up in scenic Scotland and had to leave at short notice. Ruth shook her head. Ben had never been the most organised of people, so it didn't say much if him leaving made life more complicated! She pursed her lips, determined to rediscover the old Ruth, who was capable and strong; the woman who looked for the positives in life.

Ellie dug her hand into her skirt pocket, pulled out a fifty pence piece and brandished it like a magic coin. 'I didn't spend all my money at the end-of-year fair today. Let's walk over to the corner shop. At least we can get some sweets.'

Ruth went back to the front seat and rummaged around in the glove compartment. She emerged with a one pound coin and smiled. 'This might buy us a drink. We can feast on the picnic food when we get back home. I'll set it all up, in the back garden.'

With a lopsided grin, Ellie grabbed Ruth's hand. 'I'm dying to paddle in the river, Mum. My toes have felt hot and sticky all day, even though we had our lessons under the shade of the big oak tree.'

'I can't believe you'll be in the top class of Juniors next year,' said Ruth, as they crossed the road.

'It'll be so cool. Year Six get to go into lunch early and

can be play-leaders. I hope I get chosen.'

Ruth smiled as Ellie pushed open the shop's door. Her daughter had never been one to shirk responsibility. In fact she'd often had to encourage her to go out to play, instead of dusting the lounge or offering to re-organise the cutlery drawer. The little girl never forgot to clean out her hamster's cage and was captain of the school netball team. Ruth's chest glowed warm as her daughter paid the shopkeeper and said thank you. She was just like her dad, who'd helped out at Scouts and been a school governor.

Fifteen minutes later they were sharing a juice and sucking on fruit pastilles by the river bank. Socks and shoes off, Ellie's legs hung down into the cool water, feet submerged amongst laces of weed. Ruth had kicked off her high heels and rolled up her blouse sleeves. Face tilted back, she closed her eyes and hoped the sun might erase the dark circles she'd acquired from the recent months of sleepless nights.

'Look, a ladybird!' Ellie turned around raised her hand to her mum. The lipstick-red creature strolled across her little palm before flying off.

'The river smells musty today,' Ruth said, eyes open now.

'Reminds me of Dad's socks, after he's played a game of squash.' Ellie fiddled with her ponytail. 'Can we go to, um, see him again, this weekend?'

Ruth sat up and nodded. No doubt Ellie would draw a picture to put at his graveside, like last time.

Ellie turned back to the water. 'So, Uncle Ben definitely won't want his fancy telly, up in Scotland?'

'No – he's kindly left it for us.' Ruth reached forward and squeezed her daughter's shoulder. 'In any case, I don't think it would fit in his new flat.'

Ellie got up and sat next to her mum. She crossed her wet legs.

'I'll miss him,' the little girl said.

'All this – Uncle Ben moving away... Us living on our own... Don't worry,' said Ruth, in a bright voice. 'It's just a period of adjustment.'

Ellie's brow furrowed.

'What I mean is... For a while everything will be different, but soon we'll settle into a new routine.' Ruth cleared her throat. 'So... What lessons did you have, today...?'

It was difficult to know what would upset Ellie more – discussing Uncle Ben leaving or changing the subject. He'd been such a support since Gavin's illness, having moved in towards the end, to help out in any way he could. As a determined older sister, Ruth would never have thought that one day she'd be depending on her younger sibling.

'We've been studying seasons around the world, all week,' said Ellie, 'and today Miss Jones asked us to write down the best bits of each one in England. I was surprised, 'cos even though I don't like autumn and winter as much, I could still find good things to say.'

'Which is your favourite season?'

'Summer - ice-cream's my number one thing!' said Ellie, voice more upbeat now. 'Also, trips to the beach and the smell of cut grass.' She grinned. 'Daddy listening to football on his radio in the garden, and shouting so loud that you and me hear the neighbours complain.'

'What did you find to like about autumn, then?' Ruth plucked a long blade of grass and slid it between her teeth.

'Well, at first it's colder and the nights start getting

dark. But then all the leaves fall off the trees, in well cool colours – orange, red and gold. There's Halloween… Remember when Dad dressed up as the Grim Reaper and Lucy from next door rang the front door bell?'

'She dropped her broom when he shouted mwahahaaaa!' Ruth's face broke into a smile.

Ellie giggled. 'I also love Bonfire Night and circling Sparklers in the air.' She cocked her head. 'Then there's winter and lots of indoor lunchtimes at school, cos it's raining. But after a few weeks pretty frost patterns decorate cars. Everything turns white, like someone from outer space has a massive cereal box full of snowflakes and is shaking it upside down. And there's Christmas…' She sighed. 'Chocolate logs, fairy lights, pretty baubles and opening presents… Mum?' Her voice shrank, for a second. 'What will happen this Christmas…? Us waking up without Dad…?'

Ruth swallowed hard and wished she had all the answers. Gavin had been gone since January. This would be the first festive season since. 'I don't know, but I promise we'll try to make it great.' A lump rose in her throat as she and Ellie both watched a bumble bee home in on a wild flower. 'So…That leaves spring,' she said, eventually, in control of the unexpected surge of grief she'd felt, at the thought of eating turkey and pulling crackers, without her husband.

Ellie nodded. 'Fluffy chicks on the river, banana coloured daffodils and yummy Easter eggs.'

The two of them put on their shoes, stood up and headed for a little bridge that arched over the babbling water. Ellie picked up two twigs.

'Beat you at Pooh Sticks, Mum!'

This was her dad's game – oh the hollers when Ellie's

twig swept under the bridge first, before his. Mother and daughter dropped theirs onto the water, then lunged to the other side of the bridge and gazed down.

'Yay!' Ellie punched the air.

'Again!' said Ruth and this time she won - but not the next time, nor the one after that. 'I give in,' she chuckled. 'Come on. Let's go home. I'm baking hot.'

Hand-in-hand, they walked in silence, passing toddlers on swings and listening to a dog bark.

'The changing of seasons,' said Ellie, all of a sudden, 'it's a bit like our family.'

'I suppose it is,' said Ruth, softly. 'So which season are we approaching at the moment?'

She was sure Ellie would say they'd still be stuck in winter for a while, now that her favourite Uncle was disappearing up north. Most of the time, her little girl was too good at putting on a brave face, something else she got from her dad. How brave he'd been, telling the family about his diagnosis. Gavin always had a smile for Ellie, even towards the end. Although he would have said that Ellie's nerve came from her mum. Ruthless Ruth, he used to teasingly call her, when they first started dating and she was hitting her targets as a sales executive.

'We're heading into spring,' Ellie said. 'Winter's passing, I think...' A funny noise rattled in her throat.

'What is it, love?' asked Ruth and stopped still, her daughter's face hidden under the sunhat.

'Getting used to Daddy not stealing my chips or telling bad jokes...It's made me feel cold inside.'

Ruth knelt down, lifted her daughter's chin and stared straight into her eyes. 'Me too, darling.' She slipped her arms around Ellie and gave her a big hug.

'Ellie!'

They both looked up. Another girl ran over, followed by her dad. Ruth vaguely recognized her as Megan, one of her daughter's friends from Girl Guides.

'Come and look at some frogs I've spotted,' said Megan.

Ellie's mouth upturned and she looked at her mum.

'Just quickly then,' said Ruth with a smile.

'Lovely weather, isn't it?' said Megan's Dad, as the two girls ran off. 'Let's hope it stays with us until September.'

'Yes. We're not going away this summer, so I hope it doesn't rain for the whole of August, like last year.'

He grinned. 'We're off to Spain, which knowing my luck means you'll have a heatwave here, and my wife and I will have spent all that money for nothing.'

Ruth bit her lip. Lucky Megan. From now on Ellie would only holiday with one parent.

'In fact, we're off to the swimming pool now, so that Megan can test out her new costume!' he said, as the girls arrived back, gasping with laughter. 'It's a special, end-of-term inflatable session, for Under Elevens.'

'You should come, Ellie,' said Megan. 'We could meet you there.'

Ellie's face lit up. 'Ooh, could we, Mummy?'

'It starts at five,' said Megan's dad and consulted his watch. 'In fact, it's time to get going.'

Ellie raised her eyebrows and Ruth grinned. An inflatable session would be a proper end-of-year treat.

'We'd better hurry, then, darling and pick up your swimsuit from home,' said Ruth. 'Swimming will build up a good appetite for our picnic!'

They promised to see Megan later at the pool and headed for the car.

'Nice girl,' said Ruth.

'Megan's parents are divorced,' said Ellie. 'Her dad got married again.'

'Oh? I just assumed…'

'She doesn't keep getting into trouble, any more, like she did when her Mum and Dad first broke up. Now she's a patrol leader.' Ellie thought for a moment. 'Perhaps we'll be all right, too. Like you say, Mum – it's a period of…'justment.'

They turned towards the car park, both of them squinting in the sun. Ruth caught sight of their shadows on the tarmac. They were hand-in-hand as ever, but for just one fleeting second, Ellie's looked like the tall, wise grown-up one.

12
LUCK O' THE IRISH

Bar manager, Shane, entered the room and frowned. This made him no less attractive to Jenny, who stopped cleaning tables for a moment, to admire his striking, marine-blue eyes. When dozing off, at night, she could picture every curve, every freckle of his face. Jenny smiled at him, a familiar wave of pain squeezing her chest. Unrequited love was a cruel thing. Even if he had been interested, the bar manager strongly discouraged relationships between staff at the Rising Sun– ever since two bartenders had split up and argued in front of customers.

'Now, how are you, this afternoon, Jenny? Looks like you're doing a grand job,' he said.

'Thanks, Shane.' Jenny's heart skipped a beat. 'Everything all right with you?' She set down her dishcloth and bacterial spray and tucked a loose black curl behind her ear.

'Talk about the luck o' the Irish – the fiddler I'd booked for tonight has just rung. He's sprained his wrist, so he has. How do we celebrate St Patrick's Day without folk music?'

Jenny shrugged. 'I'm sure we could find a suitable CD to play – perhaps you've got one at home, what with you coming from the emerald isle.' She grinned. 'And don't forget us staff are wearing our green ties and earrings.

Plus, today's special is Irish stew.'

Shane's eyes crinkled at the corners. 'That's what I like about you, Jenny – you're always so positive. Yes, the food should be grand, since I've given me mam's fail-safe recipe to our new chef.'

Jenny nodded and rubbed her damp hands against her jeans. Shane often talked about his family and made trips home. As he listed the ingredients, his gentle, Irish lilt, as usual, made Jenny tingle. Yet her chest uncontrollably squeezed again. Shane wouldn't think her so positive if he knew how hopelessly she loved him.

'It's, um, really important to you, isn't it,' she said, 'that tonight's takings are up?'

'Of course – thanks to the recession, we rely on these special occasions more than ever. At least Frances was pleased with our income over Christmas. Plus Valentine's Day went well and Mothering Sunday, last week.' He shrugged. 'When the brewery took me on, I promised to turn this place around. It's important I keep my word.'

Jenny bit her lip. Frances, the area manager, had visited much more than usual, during the last month or so. What with her flawless make-up and tailored trouser suits, Shane seemed to have taken a real shine to her. He'd serve Frances lunch in the pub's most private corner and the two of them would talk non-stop. By the number of times they laughed, their discussions must have covered more interesting topics than stock-taking and brands of beer.

Shane sat down at the table Jenny had been cleaning and stretched out his legs.

'Would you mind nipping into town,' he said, 'to see if the supermarket has any bright green serviettes? Our usual supplier didn't have any. Otherwise we'll use our regular white ones.'

Jenny nodded. 'So, what about the music?'

'You're probably right - I'm bound to have something in my collection at home. Later on, I'll pay my flat a quick visit.' He ran a hand over the smooth, mahogany table top. 'And do whatever you can to spread word of tonight's celebrations, won't you, now, Jenny? Whilst you're out I'll ask Adrian to help me put up the decorations.'

She raised her eyebrows.

'I ordered some huge green cardboard shamrocks off the internet,' he said and chuckled. 'Talk about clichés! Although I'm hoping they might bring us some luck.'

'And the extra delivery of Guinness arrived?'

'Sure did. At least most of the evening's preparations are going to plan.' He crossed his fingers. 'Please, universe – no more bad luck!'

'You know I'll do what I can, to help,' said Jenny and the two of them gazed at each other for a second, his frown now disappeared. Despite longing to eke out the moment, Jenny wanted to make sure the evening was a success. She grabbed her coat and headed off down the high street. It was late afternoon and as Jenny passed the travel motel, two animated men with Geordie accents came out. The tallest bumped into her.

'Ee, sorry lass,' he said. 'I wasn't looking. Me mind's still full of yesterday's footie match. Newcastle United were on reet good form!'

'We were just dissecting the team's tactics,' said the other man and grinned.

Jenny pictured Shane sighing about the injured fiddler and took a deep breath. 'You could carry on the celebrations, this evening,' she said and returned the grin.

'The Rising Sun, where I work, down the road, is hosting a St Patrick's Day night, with bargain stew and Guinness. Why don't you come along?'

'Ee, that's a canny idea,' said the taller man 'We've just arrived for a conference here, tomorrow, and the motel does seem a bit quiet… Thanks for the tip, lass.'

'See you later, then,' said Jenny, feeling pleased with herself. At least that would bring in some extra custom. Humming now, she turned into the supermarket and walked up and down the aisles, looking for serviettes. A woman in a striking purple coat, reached up for a big red tub of salt. Somehow it slipped through her fingers, whizzed past her left ear and fell on the floor. Jenny stopped to pick it up.

'Thanks, dear,' muttered the woman. 'I'm getting in supplies for tonight, just in case anyone tips red wine on my cream carpet. Apparently a good shake of salt helps absorb such spillages.'

'You're having a party?' said Jenny.

'Not really – my husband's archery pals are coming over to discuss how to commemorate their centenary, later this year. They were due to hold the meeting in the archery hut, but due to all that rain last night, it's flooded. My husband generously said not to cancel – that I'd be happy to put on some drinks and nibbles.' She rolled her eyes.

'Oh dear,' said Jenny.

The woman smiled. 'Ach, just ignore me – it's not really his fault. I've been on at him for months to have his archery friends over. He only joined the club last year, when he retired. I would have just liked a bit more notice!' she said.

'Well, if it's any help, I've got a suggestion,' said Jenny.

'The Rising Sun is hosting an Irish night with Guinness and stew, to celebrate St Patrick's Day. It might prove to be a good meeting place for your husband and his friends.' Jenny shrugged. 'You could suggest that they bring their wives along.'

'What a great idea!' said the woman, the creases in her face immediately smoothing out.

Jenny beamed as the woman hurried away, already dialing a number on her mobile phone. Hopefully a bustling pub, tonight, would put the usual charming smile back onto gorgeous Shane's face. Jenny paid for the serviettes and began the trek back to the pub. She admired the outline of a horse, in the twilight, up ahead. It was trotting near to the kerb, a young man on top of it, in a reflective jacket. Suddenly the horse stumbled. Jenny hurried over. It looked as if the back foot had got stuck in some thick mud.

Keeping away from its rear legs, Jenny bent down and picked up a horseshoe. It must have twisted off. She held it out to the man who had dismounted.

'Cheers,' he said and shook his head. 'This shoe must have already been loose. What great timing. I'm supposed to be doing a Sunday roast for my girlfriend, tonight, and am already late. Now I'll have to give his hoof the once over, as well, when I get back to the stables.'

Jenny smiled to herself through the darkness. Could he be another customer, perhaps? It certainly seemed so, when she mentioned the Irish themed night. The man's face lit up and he said his girlfriend loved Irish stew and was bound to want to go out instead.

Thrilled, Jenny said her goodbyes and rushed back to the pub.

'Wow!' she said, on pushing open the door. Huge

green, cardboard shamrocks hung from the ceiling.

'Pretty grand, eh?' said Shane, as he came over to take the bag of serviettes. He glanced at her hand. 'What's that?'

She looked down. Urgh! The muddy horseshoe! In her hurry, she'd forgotten to give it to the young man.

'Don't hold it upside down,' said Shane. 'All of the luck will tip out.'

'You may believe in all that nonsense, but I don't need luck to help me drum up business,' said Jenny, with a comical smug smile. She took off her coat and proceeded to tell him about her trip to the supermarket.

As she finished, Shane started to laugh, blue eyes twinkling like waves rippling under the sun.

'What's so funny?' she said.

'You? Not need luck?' he said. 'So tell me, do you know what they call Newcastle United fans?

'Magpies – because of their black and white strip,' she said. That bit of trivia she knew, thanks to her football-mad dad.

'Precisely,' he said. 'You saw two of them – that's lucky, ask anyone. As for the lady in the supermarket... Am I right in thinking the salt flew over her left shoulder?'

Laughing with him now, Jenny nodded. Of course – another omen of good luck.

'Then there was the horseshoe,' she said, before he could carry on.

Shane clapped his hands. 'Wouldn't it be grand if all those people actually turned up?' He patted her shoulder. 'You've done the Rising Sun proud, Jenny. Well done for taking the initiative and trying to make tonight a success.' He cleared his throat. 'Talking of good fortune, erm, there's something I want to talk to you about, tonight, when Frances is here.'

Jenny swallowed hard. What was this – some sort of joint announcement from Shane and Frances? A shiver crossed Jenny's spine. Were her worst fears about to come true? Had he fallen for the dynamic, fashionable area manager? At that moment the other bartender, Adrian, came up from the cellar.

'We'll talk later, Jenny, so we will,' said Shane, and stared at her for a moment, before heading to the kitchen with the bag of serviettes.

Cheeks flushed, she stood fixed to the spot and raised a hand to where he'd touched her shoulder. Her chest squeezed. Sometimes she could hardly bear their time together. It was torture to hide her true feelings. But there was no point thinking like that - especially with so much work to be done before opening time; especially as Shane had once said he'd never date someone who worked alongside him.

She pursed her lips. Glamorous Frances probably didn't count as she was based at the brewery's headquarters. Perhaps lovely Shane had been dating her already and after a whirlwind romance, the important announcement involved a ring and church?

Blocking such thoughts from her mind, Jenny headed for the bar. Nope. Get a grip. Stop being paranoid. He'd simply mentioned "good fortune" – perhaps the brewery was going to give Jenny a pay rise? Maybe finally they could offer her the extra hours she'd been asking for? Jenny had been lucky to get this temporary job, three months ago, but was desperate for something permanent or at least a bigger weekly income.

Several hours later, she was still pondering her future, a splash of Guinness on her green tie, one Leprechaun earring almost falling out. The night had gone better than anyone could have imagined, plus both magpies, the salt lady with the archery club and horseman plus girlfriend had turned up! Shane had winked at Jenny across the room, as people clapped to his CD of Irish jigs. What a fab evening! Until glamorous Frances turned up and became the focus of Shane's attention.

As usual, the area manager and Shane disappeared into the corner, this time with two bowls of stew and glasses of lemonade. After a few minutes in her company, Shane had the biggest smile across his face. Jenny's stomach pinched. He was clearly thrilled about something.

'Jenny?' he said, just after the last customer left. 'Come and join Frances and me. We'd like a quick word.'

Jenny took a deep breath, put down the pint jars she was collecting and sat down in the corner, opposite them both. Adrian was cashing up and the rest of the staff was busy cleaning, in the kitchen. Shane exchanged looks with Frances.

'You may have been wondering why Frances has visited more often than usual, this last month or so,' he said. 'The truth is she and I have...'

Jenny's heart lurched. Don't be silly. If they were dating or even about to announce a more serious commitment, why would they tell her? Shane's personal relationship with the area manager was none of Jenny's business...

'The truth is,' continued Shane, 'we've been discussing the future of the brewery's local outlets. Frances is shaking things up. So, first things first... Tonight was a great success. Thanks – your hard work is really appreciated. What's more, that archery club have decided to hire our private room, out the back, and celebrate their centenary here.'

Frances nodded. 'Well said. You're a hard worker, Jenny. That's why the brewery would like to offer you a permanent position. We think you've got great potential.'

'Really?' Jenny smiled, with delight at her new job and relief – there'd been no mention of an imminent marriage! 'I mean… Thank you so much. That's brilliant news.'

'Of course, this is only possible because someone is leaving and we've taken their departure as an opportunity to re-organise.' Frances smiled at Shane. 'I'll leave your manager to explain. Goodbye Jenny. Keep up the good work. No doubt I'll be seeing you again, soon.'

Shane stood up and saw Frances to the door. Then, having locked up, he came back to the table and sat down. Jenny's cheeks flushed, as he leant forward, to gently adjust one of the Leprechaun earrings. So, the good news was the offer of a permanent position, which would mean more hours - but at what cost to someone else? Who on earth was leaving, and why?

Shane ran a finger around the top of his lemonade glass. 'Frances wanted to speak to you personally, Jenny – she seems very impressed. But, well, I guess you're wondering what this is really all about? In short, it's my hours behind the bar, you'll now take on.'

'Why?'

He grinned. 'Frances has been really pleased with the financial state of the Rising Sun and has just confirmed that she's offering me a new position – to take over the Black Griffin, in town.'

Jenny's mouth fell open. 'Wow! Congratulations! Everyone knows that's the brewery's showcase pub. The restaurant's massive and haven't they just had a makeover?'

'So, they have. No arguments, there, it's a grand place to work - and a step up the career ladder for me, so I'm really chuffed.' He grinned again. 'I must ring me mam.'

Jenny nodded, pleased for him and pleased for herself – professionally speaking, that was. He'd done well, but she wasn't surprised. Shane was only a few years older than her, but back in Ireland, had grown up with parents running a village pub. What's more, he was always the first one in and last out at night. She beamed and listened to his excited plans. Yet, suddenly she noticed how her mouth felt dry and a wave of nausea had constricted her throat. And then it hit her: Shane had a new job. He'd be leaving the Rising Sun – leaving her.

'I… I really appreciate going permanent,' she eventually mumbled.

'I haven't told you the best part of it all, yet.' His voice wavered slightly, as he reached out a hand and slid his fingers in between hers. 'Sweet Jenny… All this time, I've been longing to get to know you better. And now finally, we won't be colleagues, so there's nothing to stop me from asking you out.'

Jenny digested this news for a minute, like the mental equivalent of a double-take. Eyes all shiny, she squeezed his fingers tight.

'How about a curry, tomorrow night?' he said. 'Unless… I mean, of course, if you're not interested…' He bit his lip.

'That would be lovely,' she said, a warm glow spreading across her chest. Was this really happening, after all these weeks of telling herself not to think of Shane as anything but her boss?

'That's grand!' he murmured and gently kissed her

cheek. 'Maybe us Irish are lucky, after all!'

13

CHASING RAINBOWS

Tom helped Anna into her polka dot boots and pink anorak. Baby in her arms, his wife, Ruby, hovered a few feet away.

'Tom, don't be like this,' she said, blue eyes twinkling. 'You know I'm always right.'

'Not this time, love. In my humble opinion, our budget just won't stretch to a holiday this year - especially now that we've got two children.' He straightened up. 'George needs nappies like they're going out of fashion and the car's hardly new. On top of daily spends, we need something in the bank, for a rainy day.'

Mouth now set in a firm line, Ruby rocked baby George. 'But we agreed, when we had Anna, that we'd always make two weeks away, as a family, a priority. What with the long hours you've been working, surely it's more important than ever?' She shrugged. 'Somehow we'll find the money – we always do.'

'How exactly?' Tom raised his eyebrows. 'We're still paying off last summer's fortnight in Spain. I warned you, one way or another you'd regret all those glasses of Sangria.'

'Speak for yourself! I was still pregnant with George, if you remember, and stuck to lemonade.'

The couple smiled at each other.

'Anyway, you said yourself that food prices keep

going up,' he continued. 'Christmas nearly broke the bank, plus Anna's just started those horse-riding lessons…'

'I could find out about those work-from-home schemes – you know, stuffing envelopes.'

'Most of those are scams nowadays, I've heard,' said Tom and lifted up his rucksack.

'A… a paper-round, then. You don't leave for work until eight. I'm awake early with George, anyway. Gill's son earns one hundred pounds a month, doing his. Add that up, over the year-'

'You'd be even more exhausted than you are now, love,' said Tom.

Ruby's eyes crinkled at the corners. 'Okay, then – how about I become a kissogram, like your brother's last girlfriend?'

Tom rolled his eyes. 'Look, you're busy enough looking after the children, Ruby.'

'It was a joke…' Her shoulders sagged. 'Fine, if you're not even prepared to discuss the options…'

At that moment, Anna looked up from fiddling with her zip. Ruby fixed a big smile on her face.

'Have a lovely walk with Daddy, darling,' she said. 'Remember to put up your hood, if it rains – the forecast is showery.'

'Okay, Mummy.' Anna darted forward and gently patted George's tiny hand, before going to the front door.

'Look, I don't want to fall out – let's discuss the holiday later, Ruby…' mumbled Tom.

'Don't worry about it – you're probably right,' she said in a resigned voice and turned around to take George upstairs. 'By the way, if I'm not here when you get back, I'll be at Mum's.'

An hour later, in the middle of a big field, Tom still felt heavy inside. He hated arguing with Ruby, especially as it didn't happen very often. What's more, he knew, deep down, that she really was right. Since George was born last November, and Anna started the top year at infants, both he and Ruby were continually shattered. George didn't sleep well and cried for England, whereas Anna's life had become a whirlwind of after-school clubs and tea invitations. As for Tom's job, the demands were higher than ever. Sales targets had increased, even though selling savings policies had never been more challenging, thanks to the recession. By the summer, he and Ruby would both badly need a change of scene...

'Daddy, it's raining and sunny at the same time!'

'So it is, sweetheart,' he said and put up Anna's hood. 'Come on, let's head for those big evergreen trees, over by that turnstile - the ground might be dry underneath.'

Holding hands, they rushed through the lush grass, Anna giggling as her boots squelched through patches of mud. Finally, cheeks speckled with wet drops, Tom and Anna took refuge under the evergreen trees' thick branches. He took a plastic sheet out from his rucksack.

'Sit on this, Anna. I'll get out our sandwiches.' Tom rubbed his hands. There was a distinct chill in the air. 'Are you sure you don't want to go back and eat in the car?'

'No! You promised we'd have proper picnic, Daddy.'

He grinned. 'So I did.'

Minutes later, the rain had stopped again and they sat munching egg and cress sandwiches – Anna's favourites because they were Granny's favourites too.

'I love picnics,' said Anna. 'Look, Daddy – that cow's watching us.'

Tom glanced across to the neighbouring field.

'Do you think he likes egg?' asked Anna.

'No more than Mummy,' said Tom and they both laughed.

Ruby hated the smell of egg, yet insisted on cooking Anna her favourite sandwich filling. That was the kind of mum she was, thought Tom – selfless; caring.

'Mummy prefers cheese with Marmite,' said Tom, as sun broke through the cloud and added some shine to a nearby puddle. He and Anna exchanged looks and pulled faces. Ruby had some strange eating habits – mashed banana on toast, salad for breakfast… It was one of the quirkier things about her that Tom had always loved.

'Come on,' he said, when they'd finished their homemade chocolate muffins. 'Let's go over and say hello to that cow.

They stood up and brushed off crumbs before Anna squealed.

'So, pretty! Daddy, look at that rainbow!'

Tom stopped folding the plastic sheet for a moment and gazed into the sky. Wow. It looked as if someone had brushed a multi-coloured highlighter pen across the chink of blue sky.

'It's magical…' muttered Anna. 'Which colour do you like best, Daddy? I love the orange.'

'The blue,' said Tom. 'It exactly matches Mummy's eyes.'

'Let's try to find the end of it.' Anna clapped her hands.

'It could be a long walk.'

'Pleeeeease! There might be buried treasure.'

Gold coins would come in handy, if we're going away this year, thought Tom. He ruffled Anna's copper curls.

'Okay, sweetheart – but it might be further away, than

you expect.'

'Yay!' Anna punched the air before trudging in the direction of the fluorescent arc. However, twenty minutes later her trudging had slowed to a stroll.

'The end isn't any nearer, Daddy,' she said, bottom lip jutting out. 'Chasing rainbows is a tiring business.'

'It is,' said Tom and chuckled at her grown-up sounding sentence. 'But that's the magic of rainbows - they are never-ending.' He took off his rucksack and reached in for the empty, Tupperware sandwich box. 'I've got an idea. This can be a treasure chest. Why don't we fill it with precious things we can find here and take it back for Mummy, as a present?'

Anna nodded vigorously, took the box and scoured the ground, whilst Tom slipped his rucksack on again. Perhaps he could get some overtime, to pay for a holiday. He'd tell Ruby when he got home – if she was there. His stomach twisted. What if she'd meant she was actually moving out to live with her mum?

Tom shook himself. Don't be silly! Talk about paranoid! Despite the recent sleepless months of frayed tempers, things weren't that bad. Although colicky George took so long to settle that Tom and Ruby had regularly turned down offers of babysitting. This meant it was months since they'd been out alone together for a coffee, let alone a romantic, candlelit meal.

Ruby – his Ruby, gem by name, gem by nature... That's what he always used to whisper in her ear. Who needed to chase rainbows, with a wife like her? Tom swallowed. It was hard to imagine life without Ruby. He shouldn't have been so negative about her ideas on how to earn extra money. Goodness knows she deserved putting her feet up for two weeks of the year.

'Look at this cute ladybird, Daddy!' Carefully Anna dropped the blood-red beetle into the box.

'Let's put some leaves in for it,' said Tom. 'We can let it go in our back garden, later. Have you spotted any other treasures?'

Anna picked up a small shiny black stone and put that in too. They walked a bit further, near to a row of pine trees, and with a whoop, Anna collected several cones.

'Daisies!' she then cried, and pointed to a patch of short grass Tom helped her string together a chain of the delicate flowers, which Anna carefully placed in the box.

'Clover – that's lucky!' she announced. 'We could pick lots to take home – Mummy could look through them and might find a four-leaved one.'

'Good idea,' said Tom and glanced at a nearby gorse bush, with its vibrant yellow flowers. He smiled to himself. "Gorse in bloom means it's the kissing season, m'laddo," his granddad used to say, every winter.

'Come on, Anna,' Tom mumbled, stomach tingling. 'Let's get back to your Mum. The rainbow's gone and those clouds look dark.'

'Do you think she'll like her present?'

Tom nodded and took Anna's hand. 'I think she'll love it.' Ruby wasn't the materialistic sort and would be thrilled with nature's jewels, as if they were the real McCoy.

'Ruby?' Tom called as they went in the front door. His heart raced as there was no reply. Yawning, Anna squidged off her boots and let her anorak fall to the floor. Sternly, Tom raised one eyebrow at her and with a giggle, she picked it up and handed it to him to slip over one of the coat pegs, on the wall.

'Mummy!' shouted Anna. 'We've got something for

you.'

Silence. Tom's mouth went dry.

'Hurry up, Mummy!' insisted Anna.

Finally someone hissed 'Shhh...' from upstairs. Seconds later, Ruby crept down, a finger to her upturned mouth. 'George has just settled for his nap. Let's go into the lounge.'

Relief surging through his veins, Tom kissed her on the cheek.

'You and me... Are we all right?' he whispered, as they followed Anna into the living room.

Ruby paused and theatrically cocked her head. 'No, we're half left.'

'Ha, ha,' he said and grinned at the family joke they shared.

'Right, what's this present then?' said Ruby, as she and Tom sat on the sofa.

Anna handed her the box. 'We chased a pretty rainbow, Mummy, but couldn't reach the end to dig for treasure, so we've filled our own chest.'

Ruby prised off the lid and one by one picked up all the objects, apart from the ladybird.

'What a beautiful necklace,' she said and lay the daisy chain on her lap. 'And I love the feel of soft clover, especially if I walk on it in bare feet.'

'We could look for a four-leaved one,' said Anna.

Ruby grinned. 'Of course – go up to Mummy and Daddy's room, darling, and fetch my magnifying glass from the second drawer down, next to the bed.'

The little girl scooted out of the room and Ruby smiled at Tom.

'Sorry about before - I know you're under a lot of pressure at work,' she said.

'No, it's me who should apologise.' Tom squeezed her arm. 'You were right, of course. We need that fortnight every summer, away from the daily routine. Perhaps I can get some overtime.'

'No. You work hard enough,' said Ruby. 'Anyway I might have the solution. Whilst you were out, I paid Mum a visit. Jean, a friend of hers, has just bought a caravan in Wales. Mum mentioned it last week.'

Tom sat more upright and nodded.

'Apparently Jean's looking to rent it out, when she's not there herself,' continued Ruby. 'She'd probably offer us mates' rates. Mum gave me her phone number. It's on a site with a swimming pool and kids entertainment.' Ruby beamed. 'What do you think? I'm sure with a bit of forward-planning, we could afford that. We don't need a fancy holiday abroad – as long as we're all together'

Tom put his hands on her shoulders. 'Ruby, you really are a gem by name and gem by nature. It's a brilliant idea, love. And it means you won't have to work as a kissogram.' He grinned. 'Unless you want to, when you're sitting next to your husband.'

Eyes twinkling, she slid her arms around his waist and Tom's stomach tingled as their lips met. His granddad must have been right about gorse in bloom bringing on the kissing season.

14
THE LAST DANCE

Susie took a deep breath and glanced at herself in the mirror. High heels and sequins weren't too much for a woman pushing sixty, she decided, but perhaps a bit over-the-top for a grocer. She was more used to wearing fingerless gloves, a woolly hat and windcheater. Side-to-side she turned. Needs must, as tonight she was determined to… well, *hoped* to, at least… get closer to charming Dirk.

As she left the cloakroom, and hovered by the scout hut kitchens, Susie smiled to herself. Who was she kidding? When it came to what her young grandson called "icky love stuff", she felt like a clumsy teenager. Plus since Bob had died, she'd thought about nothing but their life together. Until Dirk moved into the area, that is, a few months ago; until she'd encountered his infectious laugh and generous nature.

'He's as smooth as one of my Cappucino truffles,' Marilyn had said at the last meeting of LO-BIZ, a committee of local business people. 'I can't wait to dance with him at our fund-raising New Year's Eve ball.' Marilyn was the owner of *Chocs Away*, one of the most successful shops in the village. She'd made it no secret that she had her eye on the handsome newcomer.

Susie sighed for a moment, imagining being whisked around the dance floor, by kind, capable Dirk. With his chestnut eyes and grey-streaked copper hair, he was tall, dark, good-looking – to be honest, a bit of a cliché. Not what her usual type had been at all, in the old days of courting, before she'd married Bob. Not that it was called courting in the Sixties – well, only by Susie's gran, who'd taken a while to come around to accepting Bob, with his tight-fitting Mod suits and Italian scooter!

Susie smoothed down her blue sparkly dress. No doubt glamorous Marilyn would get the last dance of the evening. Not that it mattered, Susie thought, promptly scolding herself. For goodness sake, you are a mature woman! A grandmother!

Susie peered into the dance hall. Fortunately it was a decent size, as the scout hut was the biggest building the committee could afford to hire. Smiling couples streamed past her, and whilst everyone else seemed to be in pairs, Susie had arrived on her own.

Perhaps it had been a mistake for her to come out. But then her daughter, Ann, and her family were skiing abroad. Susie had been lucky enough to spend Christmas and Boxing day with them and Ann had her own life to lead. That was the good thing about LO-BIZ - it gave Susie plenty to think about, apart from her job at the grocer's.

So enough of being silly - this dance was for a good cause. Plus she'd scrubbed up well enough, or so Wolfie, her Labrador had said. He'd barked his approval anyway. How Bob used to chuckle when Susie insisted she and the dog understood each other's thoughts.

'Evening, Susie! Don't you look lovely?' said a warm voice, just audible above the laughter and Big Band music wafting out of the hall. Oh dear – what an annoying time for a hot flush to strike. Stomach fluttering, she turned around.

'Oh, hello Dirk. You, um, look jolly smart, too.'

But then Dirk always looked sharply dressed, when he visited her grocer's shop on weekday lunchtimes. In fact she'd never seen him out of a suit, as he came to the LO-BIZ meetings straight from work. Not that she was complaining - how dashing he looked tonight, in his tuxedo. And what an asset he'd been to the committee, with his finance company footing the bill for the ball's posters and tickets. He'd even sorted out the license from the local council, so that they could sell alcohol.

Chestnut eyes crinkling at the corners, he grinned.' I almost didn't recognize you, without your stripy scarf on.'

Susie grinned back. 'Yes, sorry – I haven't got a secret stash of your favourite Brussel Sprouts to hand, either. Not even those fancy purple ones.'

Dirk pulled a face – he was clearly a traditionalist, when it came to food.

For a few seconds, they stood smiling, in a comfortable silence, which was… nice. With Dirk, Susie felt she could always be herself. Whilst she bagged his runner beans or apples, they often chatted about well… nothing much important, maybe the news or weather. What mattered was that she felt at ease, whether they laughed together, rolled their eyes, or said nothing at all.

'You've done a fantastic job, setting up,' he said eventually. 'It's a shame I had to nip into the office and couldn't help out.'

Susie blushed. 'Thanks. It took all afternoon. We never thought we'd spruce this old hut up in time. We've scrubbed, dusted, hung plastic mistletoe and arranged chairs in friendly circles… '

'Did Marilyn's wine merchant friend deliver the drink, all right?'

Susie nodded. 'And Mr Watson's son arrived early to set up his DJ equipment. So far everything's gone to plan. Plus, today we sold the last ticket.'

Dirk let out a low whistle. 'That's fantastic. Tonight should raise enough to really improve the village playground.'

'Cooeeee! Diirrrrrk!' called a voice and Marilyn shimmied out of the main hall. 'There you are. Come on in. There's a catchy tune playing.' Her red lips upturned further. 'Hello, Susie. You look fab!'

Susie's jaw dropped. Goodness. Marilyn had really pushed the boat out, with her black dress's slit skirt. As the chocolatier told anyone who would listen, the secret to healthily running a chocolate shop, was to work out at the gym five times a week. Indeed, despite being in her fifties, she certainly carried off the fashionable look.

Dirk strode over to Marilyn and kissed her hand. Susie's stomach twisted briefly, before she concentrated on walking carefully in her new heels. She followed the striking couple towards the music, admiring Marilyn's snug waist and toned calves. Bob always liked to think of himself as a keep-fit fanatic, and often bought new gym equipment, which always ended up in the garage, in mint condition, when the novelty quickly wore off. Susie grinned to herself. Oh how indignantly he'd blame her home-cooking for his expanding waistline, yet complain if she dared swap butter for a low-fat spread.

'Back in a moment, ladies,' said Dirk, as soon as the three of them were in the hall. He bowed and headed over to a group of people who greeted him with big smiles and claps on the back. The room was heaving already. By the time Susie had raced home after setting up, changed and returned, the party was well underway. But it had all been worth it, she thought, and stood still for a moment, admiring tables covered with gold tablecloths, with matching helium balloons, tied down, in the middle of them. Marilyn had donated enough chocolates to scatter on plates, around the room. The floor was sparkling clean and dimmed lights hid frays on the black curtains.

'You wouldn't think Dirk's only a few years off retiring,' said Marilyn, in a dreamy voice. 'He's a real dish, as my mother would have said – except that he isn't bald. Dad often teased her for her crushes on Kojak and Yul Bryner.'

Susie smiled. 'My Mum loved Gene Kelly and Howard Keel – all the musical stars…'

'What about you?' said Marilyn, swaying side-to-side now as the DJ put on a new record.

Susie's cheeks felt hot. She couldn't really remember a celebrity crush since her teenage obsession with John Lennon. Thankfully, before Marilyn could press her any further, Mr Watson came over to ask if one of them could help out in the kitchen. Glad to escape, Susie insisted she'd do it. However, just as she arrived there was a clatter and cries of despair. She walked in. Everyone was staring at the floor.

'What's the matter, Cath?' asked Susie.

'We thought of everything, apart from bringing a corkscrew,' said the young, red-headed woman. 'Fortunately we found an old one in a drawer, here – it must have been left from a previous event. I've just dropped it and the screw's come away from the handle. The bottles we've already opened will only last, ooh… half-an-hour, at the most.'

Susie thought for a moment. It was New Year's Eve – none of the shops nearby were open.

'Give me twenty minutes,' she said, finally. 'I'll nip home and get mine.'

That's if she could find it. Susie could hardly remember the last time she'd opened a bottle of wine, since she'd been on her own. It was probably a few months ago, when the family came to hers to celebrate Ann's thirty-fifth birthday.

Hurrying in her uncomfortable shoes, Susie grabbed her coat. Her home was only a ten minute walk from the guide hut and through the village, which bustled with New Year's Eve revellers. Thankfully, the corkscrew was still where Bob used to put it – nestling at the bottom of the wooden spoons jar. Wolfie barked when she'd pulled it out - as congratulations, of course.

Susie hurtled back to the hut, her left heel getting stuck between two pavement slabs just outside the barber's. With all her might, she yanked it out hard, spurred on by the thought of a queue of impatient people needing refreshments, at the guide hut serving hatch. Sure enough, when she finally got back, people, red-faced from dancing, had formed a queue. Dirk took the corkscrew from her and delivered it straight to Cath. Then he shot back, just in time to help Susie take off her coat.

'Oh, thank you.' She smiled.

'It's the least I could do. Well done for saving the day,' he said. 'Although we had another crisis, whilst you were gone – all the electrics went. It was a bit of a job, finding the fuse box!'

'Let's hope that's our lot of bad luck for the evening then,' she said, and followed him into the hall, trying to shimmy stylishly like Marilyn. Except talk about speaking too soon - her left foot felt wobbly and before she knew it, her leg gave way as the shoe's heel snapped off. Susie collapsed to the floor.

Dirk picked her up and out of nowhere Marilyn appeared. The two of them held Susie steady.

'Are you okay?' said Dirk, brow furrowed.

'Ow! Yes… I'm fine…'

'You're limping, Susie,' said Marilyn and pointed to a spare chair by the side of the room. She helped her over there whilst Dirk hunted out the first aid box.

'That's a bad sprain if ever I saw one,' he said, on his return, as black bruising quickly came up. He knelt on the floor by Susie's side, gently slid off the broken shoe and told her to move her foot in various directions. 'You've got a full range of movement,' he said. 'I don't think it's fractured. If it's anything like the sprain I had last spring, you should be fine in a couple of days.'

Hmm, the only thing really hurt is my pride, thought Susie, noticing a scuff mark down the side of her sparkly dress.

'Here,' said Marilyn, her normally buoyant voice concerned, as she held out a plate of chocolates. 'Have a couple of these. Truffles beat medicine, every time.'

'And hold this against the bruising,' said Dirk who'd popped into the kitchen for a bag of ice-cubes.

Frivolous chocolate and practical ice… Susie watched Dirk and Marilyn, as they shook their heads and discussed the evening's mishaps. Talk about opposites attracting. Perhaps they did make a good couple and really, Marilyn was a decent sort. It was probably just as well that the glam chocolate maker would get the last dance of the night – of the year - with Dirk, in a few hours' time. What will be, will be, she thought, and hobbled over to a table full of her committee friends.

Ever the gentleman, Dirk checked on her regularly, in

between mingling with guests and being dragged onto the dance floor by Marilyn.

'Phew. I'm jiggered,' he said at one point, when there was a lull in the music. Dirk sat down next to Susie and looked at his watch. 'How are you feeling now? There's not long to go, until midnight. I hope you haven't been too bored.'

'Goodness no – it's great fun watching. I've got two left feet anyway, when it comes to hitting the dance floor.'

'Me too,' groaned Dirk. 'Marilyn's feet will be covered in bruises tomorrow – but she won't take no for an answer, every time a new tune comes on.'

'You didn't, um, bring any family or friends tonight?' asked Susie. Well, it wouldn't harm to get to know him better. 'My daughter is away, so I was quite pleased when Mr Watson suggested this New Year's Eve event.'

'Your husband... Marilyn mentioned he'd been ill... Did you lose him long ago?' Dirk asked.

'Almost three years exactly.'

'I'm sorry,' he said, softly.

Susie smiled. 'I have some wonderful memories. Bob would have loved tonight although the music wouldn't have been to his taste. The swinging sixties were always his favourite era. Given the chance, he'd twist the night away!'

'The Twist always gave me an almighty stitch!' He cleared his throat. 'In actual fact I did have another invitation tonight - from my ex-wife. She always holds a big New Year's bash.'

'Oh, um, I didn't mean to pry...' Susie squirmed.

Eyes crinkling, Dirk grinned. 'No worries. We get on well enough, now. I guess the children remind us about the best bits of our marriage.' He shrugged. 'I'm just glad that after twenty years together, we've still got our friendship. But yes, without a Plus One to take to my ex's party, I jumped at the chance to help organise this ball.'

'Cooeee! Diiirrk!'

'Off you go,' said Susie and nodded to a waving Marilyn. 'Have a dance for me.'

A heavy feeling filled her chest, as Dirk made his way towards the chocolate maker. However, like a sturdy wallflower at the school prom, she put on a brave face and concentrated on the positives of the evening. It had all gone well - apart from her foot, the corkscrew and the electrics failure! And at last the run-down village playground would get a much-needed makeover.

Cath appeared at her side, wearing an anorak.

'I'm off, now, Susie. Happy New Year and I hope your sprain gets better soon.'

Susie looked up at her. 'You aren't staying until midnight?'

'No – Jack's at home with a bad cold. He insisted I come out tonight, so as not to let everyone down, but it would be nice if we could see the New Year in together. I've got half-an-hour to get home.'

'Oh, sorry, Cath, I should have noticed that he wasn't here. But of course, you must get back to your husband. Happy New Year, dear and well done for being such a help.'

Cath raised her eyebrows. 'How will you get home?'

Good question.

'I know it's early, but I'd be very happy to drop you off, if you want now,' she continued.

Susie gazed at the dance floor and at Dirk and Marilyn's happy, perspiring faces. Everyone was just about to do the Conga.

'That's kind of you. Yes please. I'll be sorry not to help tidy up afterwards, but there's no way that's possible with this foot.'

So Cath helped Susie hobble to the cloakroom, to fetch her coat and then the two of them made their way outside, to the car park. Not much later, Susie was in her hallway, joined by a very excited Wolfie, as she waved goodbye to Cath, and shut the front door.

Limping on her bandaged foot – Dirk really seemed the expert at First Aid – Susie headed into the kitchen and flicked on the kettle. She looked at the clock. It was five to twelve.

'Looks like it's just you and me, Wolfie,' she said, and poured some dog biscuits into a bowl. But his ears perked up, seconds before the doorbell rang. Susie always thought her clever mutt had either bionic hearing or a sixth sense.

Gingerly, she made her way back through the lounge. It was late, so she peered out of the front window, first. Was that Dirk in a loose fitting anorak? And he'd taken off his bow tie. What was he doing here? Her heart raced.

She hobbled into the hallway and opened the door.

'I didn't recognize you, dressed all casual,' she said.

Dirk smiled. 'I only smarten up, big time, for the office. I'm a cords and jumper man at the weekend. Anyway.' He cleared his throat and gave a sheepish smile. 'I feel like I'm looking for Cinderella who left the dance early and forgot her shoe.' He lifted up his hands which held Susie's broken high heel. 'Perhaps I should make you fit it on!'

Susie grinned. 'That would make you Prince Charming, then.' Never a truer words spoken, either, she thought and suffered one of her hot flushes. 'Thanks for bringing it around – but, um, tomorrow would have been okay. Aren't you missing all the fun?'

Dirk winced as he handed over the shoe. 'Actually, I've pulled my back a bit, doing the Conga. I went to sit down, but you'd disappeared. You didn't catch a pumpkin, home?' He chuckled.

Susie gave a giggle. 'No – Cath kindly gave me a lift back. I would have said goodbye, but you and Marilyn...'

Eyes twinkling, Dirk shook his head. 'She's a very demanding woman. It must be exhausting living with her. I wouldn't last two minutes.'

He rubbed his hands together and Susie noticed patches of frost on the lawn.

'Would you like to come in, for a hot drink?' she said.

'Erm... Well, yes, but I know it's late. I wouldn't want to put you out, Susie.'

'No, it's fine. In fact, a bit of company would be nice, to see in the New Year.'

As Dirk stepped over the front door step, Wolfie growled.

Susie laughed. 'It's okay, Wolfie. This is a friend. Why don't you show him into the lounge?'

After staring at their guest for a moment, the Labrador trotted off towards the big armchair.

'I think that means you've got to sit there,' said Susie and grinned. Poor Dirk. With his bad back, he was walking almost as awkwardly as her. So she wouldn't let him help carry in two hot chocolates and once she'd offered him some shortbread, Susie collapsed onto the sofa. Fireworks sounded outside and she looked at the clock.

'Happy New Year, Dirk,' she said. 'Here's to neither of us injuring ourselves in the next twelve months.'

He gave his infectious laugh and told her about the

time he'd broken his ankle playing football with his son. He'd spent the whole of their Spanish summer holiday, in the pool with his plastered foot sticking out. Then Susie told him how she'd ricked her neck, years ago, showing her then young daughter how to do a front forward roll. Before they knew it, the time was one o'clock.

'Well. I must get going,' said Dirk and stood up, wincing again. 'Thanks for the drink, Susie. I… I haven't enjoyed myself so much, for a long while.'

They both went into the hallway and Susie lifted his anorak from the coat stand. As she passed it to him, the jacket dropped onto the floor. When Dirk picked it up, a spray of plastic mistletoe, from the party, fell out of one pocket. Wolfie pounced on it and balancing carefully, Susie bent down and prised it from the dog's mouth.

'Oh, that… you see…' Face red, Dirk took it from her. 'Ask, me to organise a party, and I'm your man, but when it comes to… to…' He straightened up and held the mistletoe in the air between them. 'I was rather hoping… Forgive me if it's a bit forward, but…'

Susie leant forward and kissed him on the cheek.

'Happy New Year, Dirk.' Her stomach tingled, as she stood back.

Eyes all shiny, Dirk took her hand.

'I'd love to take you out to dinner, some time, Susie,' he said. 'It would be nice to see you eat vegetables instead of weighing them into bags.'

As he squeezed her fingers gently, Susie forgot her injured foot and felt like skipping around the lounge. She may not have had the last dance of the year with Dirk, but suspected the next twelve months might put that right.

15
BLUEBIRDS OF HAPPINESS

On the sofa, Billy glanced sideways at his gran. They'd been chatting about their favourite quiz show on telly. He sipped his juice and gazed out at the back garden, and the oak tree at the bottom, waving in the wind. They hadn't played cards for a while and about to ask her for a game, Billy turned back to her neat grey curls, smart blue trousers and cream blouse... Nothing about her appearance was unusual, except that the familiar cheery mouth was down-turned. The bungalow seemed so quiet without Sky.

'What are you going to do with that?' he said and nodded towards the mahogany sideboard. An empty gold-coloured birdcage sat on top.

'Your dad said something about selling it, through a website on the computer.' She stirred her cup of tea. 'I guess there's no point hanging onto it, love.'

'You definitely aren't getting another budgie?'

'No - I'm out and about more than ever, now, what with bowls and the bridge club. Then there's my flower-arranging at the church. I only took Sky on, when Mrs Smith next door died, because her daughter was allergic to birds and couldn't re-home him elsewhere.'

'It feels... strange, without him,' mumbled Billy.

Gran gave a small smile. 'Very true – and I have *so* enjoyed his company these last eighteen months, but you know me - I prefer to see birds spread their wings outside, in their natural environment, even though I used to enjoy watching Sky take his morning flight around the lounge.'

Billy smiled. That was Gran all over – no one ever bought her cut flowers, knowing she'd rather have a plant or bulbs to grow in the garden.

'Sky had a good life, though,' he said and put his drink down on the coffee table.

Gran nodded, her dangly pearl earrings swinging to and fro.

'That he did, Billy. Mrs Smith used to call him her Bluebird of Happiness and spoilt him rotten. Of course, I couldn't resist giving him treats either. I miss watching him peck at peas or a nice chunk of cucumber.' She gave a small sigh. 'No point, moping though – these things happen.'

'I'll never forget his favourite noise,' said Billy and a grin spread across his face.

They both laughed. Over the years, Mrs Smith had blown so many kisses at Sky, that he'd picked up the sound. It was his cute party trick, to show off to visitors.

'Remember that time he sat on your head,' said Billy. 'Mum said he looked like one of those fancy little wedding hats.'

'Yes, he was my personal "fascinator".' Gran's eyes glistened. 'A handsome lad, wasn't he - such a delicate shade of blue, with his snow-white head and those sharp black speckles on his wings?'

Billy studied her face, with the hazel eyes all droopy at the corners. Gran never complained about anything, but it was obvious she missed that little bird. Since Sky had died two weeks ago, every time Billy had visited, she'd seemed sort of... lost. Billy was used to Gran chatting to the budgie or mock-scolding him for kicking his seeds out of the cage, and onto the floor. Plus she was always preparing him some tasty snack, like a plump grape or slice of apple - but then Gran liked busying around things she cared for.

Billy remembered how she used to busy around Gramps, handing him drinks or the newspaper, especially when he became ill. Sky had come into her life just a month after Gramps passed on and Billy guessed she'd been happy to become busy, once more.

'How's school, anyway, love?' said Gran and passed him another ginger biscuit. 'Joined any more clubs?'

They both chuckled. Since Billy started High School last year, it had become a family joke that he had a better social life than anyone, because of all the clubs he'd joined. There was chess on Monday and creative writing Tuesday. Wednesday was gardening club, Thursday football and Friday, well – that was the only day he was free to eat chips and gravy in the canteen, with his pals.

He told Gran all about the latest story-writing competition and chess tournament. Then they discussed her birthday in a couple of weeks' time. It fell on one of the May bank holidays which would probably mean a nice pub dinner out. Gran said that there was nothing particular she wanted – *not* cut flowers, of course. Chocolates always went down well, she hinted, a twinkle in her eye. Then Gran called him cheeky for suggesting she was seventy-three. It was seventy-*two* and he shouldn't forget that every year counted, as one got older!

Eventually, a comfortable silence fell between them, as they looked out onto the garden, again, now lit up with rays of sunshine. As a worm wriggled furiously on the patio, Billy sat upright. Of course! Why hadn't he thought of this before? A brilliant idea had just come to him. He knew exactly how to cheer his grandmother up and couldn't wait to get home, to discuss it with Mum and Dad.

It would mean Gran couldn't be in the bungalow, for her birthday. Mum would have to take her shopping, whilst he and dad got to work. Stuff would need buying for the project, but they could be her presents, so that was handy…

Stomach scrunched with excitement, Billy made his excuses and kissed Gran goodbye. As fast as he could, he cycled home, rushed inside without taking his shoes off and blurted out his plan.

'Slow down!' said Mum and gave a chuckle. Go and take your trainers off, darling, and join us at the dining room table.

Minutes later, he sat down opposite them. Without saying a word, his parents listened.

'What a thoughtful, idea, darling,' said Mum, eventually.

Billy's chest glowed.

'You're right, son – Gran would love that,' said Dad and leant across the dining room table. 'And you say you're going to start a similar project in gardening club?'

'Yes! I mean, it might cost a bit…' Billy hesitated. 'But it is Gran's birthday and I'll chip in.'

Dad ruffled Billy's black curls and got out a pen and some paper, whilst Billy fetched his laptop and found the website they'd looked at in school. It was called "How to attract wild birds to your garden." As Mum made dinner, he and Dad brainstormed details.

'Right, first things first,' said Billy and stared at the screen. 'We need to set up in a safe corner of the garden.'

Dad thought for a moment. 'What about in front of the shed? We could put a bird table in the border, there – that big holly bush, to the right, near the lawn, will give some protection against roaming cats.'

'Could we buy another plant to put nearby – it says here that prickly Hawthorn is good,' said Billy. 'That'll also keep cats away and gives the birds somewhere to shelter, whilst they wait their turn.'

Dad nodded. 'Sounds sensible. What about water? Those ceramic bird baths cost rather a lot.'

Billy scrolled down the page. 'Well, Miss said something about using a dustbin lid – you turn it upside down and build it into the soil. There aren't any plants in front of that area, blocking the view - Gran could see everything from the kitchen and lounge windows.'

Gramps always did the gardening, and whilst Gran kept things tidy, she hadn't liked to go into Gramps' shed much, since he'd died – nor had she been able to face sorting through his clothes in the wardrobe. She kept vowing to take his good jumpers and coats to the charity shop. Billy had offered to help pack the dustbin bags with her but Gran never got around to the job.

At least this project would help fill the hole left by Sky. And thank goodness Dad was giving Billy a hand – Gran always said he'd inherited Gramps' green fingers. Sure enough, Mum had been really pleased with the herb garden he'd planted for her, last year.

Dad clapped him on the back. 'Great idea! That's a good website, you've found. I've got a spare lid from that bin we don't use anymore.'

'It says Elderflower is another good plant to attract birds,' said Billy. 'And how about buying Ivy or Honeysuckle to grow up the area of fence, on the nearby left?'

Dad studied the computer screen. 'If the prices aren't too steep, I don't see why not – although you realize this is a long-term project, son. Plants take time to grow big and lots of different birds won't visit straightaway – but then you know that from gardening club, I suppose…'

Billy rolled his eyes. 'Of course,' he said and Dad chuckled.

'What about food?' said Dad.

'We could hang one of those feeders, filled with seed, on the shed and then Gran could decide what to put on the table. There's a recipe here for fat cakes – she could make them in the winter…'

'And in the summer the Elderflower will provide berries,' said Dad. 'So will the Hawthorn and Holly in the autumn.'

'Sounds as if you two have thought of everything!' said Mum, as she came in, holding a tea towel. 'Dinner won't be long. Go upstairs, Billy, and wash your hands.'

As he massaged the soap between his palms, Billy couldn't stop grinning. He hoped the next two weeks would pass quickly – he couldn't wait for Gran to see her surprise…

***

Luck was on Billy's side, and the next fortnight was filled with busy school days and trips to the garden centre. The Friday before the bank holiday weekend – Gran's birthday was on the Saturday – he and Dad bought the plants and special food. Billy did his research and they chose sunflower, canary and hemp seeds. As an experiment, for the winter months, he also made some fat cakes, from various scraps of cheese and bread, sultanas, oats and melted lard. Then once Mum texted to say that she and Gran had left the bungalow and were on their way into town, he and Dad drove around and wasted no time in unloading everything and carrying it into Gran's back garden. It had just gone ten o'clock.

'Good thing you have a spare key, Dad,' said Billy as he started to dig a hole for a Hawthorn bush. The May weather was on their side and despite a slight morning chill in the air, the sky was as blue as the budgie of that name, without a wisp of cloud. 'Do you think Sky would have raised the alarm, if burglars had ever broken into Gran's bungalow?' he said.

Dad looked up from the ground, hands covered in woody-smelling soil – he was kneeling on a mat, whilst he made a wide, shallow hole for the dustbin lid. He grinned. 'What do you think?'

Billy chuckled. 'No – he would have just made his favourite noise and they'd have thought he'd blown them a kiss!' He fetched a watering can and filled it from the outside tap, before tipping water into the dustbin lid. Then he helped dad plant the Elderflower and Ivy plants. Having worked up a sweat, the two of them then enjoyed a glass of squash each with a couple of Gran's chocolate biscuits – they didn't think she'd mind.

Next Dad put the bird table in the border. A few days previously, Billy had helped him creosote it a natural shade of chestnut brown. Billy upturned a small plastic bag and peanuts and cake crumbs tumbled onto the table – Mum had made a Victoria sponge birthday cake, the night before. He took the fat cakes out of another bag, and placed them there too. Dad hung the bird feeder on a hook by the roof of the shed. A hanging basket used to be there, but since Gramps had gone, Gran had never replaced its plants.

Finally, with everything in position, they stood back to admire their work. Having lost track of time, they were surprised to realize, it was already two o'clock. They hadn't even eaten their packed sandwiches.

'Mum's just texted,' said Dad. 'They are on their way back. Quick, let's tidy up and wait out the front.'

Butterflies in his stomach, Billy nodded. Gran wouldn't believe her eyes.

In fact, they narrowed with suspicion, when Mum's car pulled up and Gran saw them standing, by her front door. She got out of the car and carrying various plastic bags, headed towards them.

'What are you two up to?' she said and eyed their soil-stained jeans.

'Can't a son and grandson come over, to wish you an enjoyable birthday?' said Dad and gave her a big hug.

Billy kissed her cheek. 'Happy Birthday, Gran,' he said. 'Did you buy anything nice?'

She nodded. 'Some new wool and we had a lovely lunch out.'

'Aren't you going to invite us in?' said Dad and gave an impish grin.

Gran laughed. 'Billy, your dad looks about ten years old and reminds me of when he was a little boy and had been up to no good. What's this all about?'

Dad took out his spare key and they went inside. Billy led Gran into the lounge and instructed her to close her eyes as they neared the window. He guided her right up to the glass pane and jerked his head excitedly at his parents – a couple of small brown birds already stood on the creosoted table.

'Right, Gran,' said Billy, 'open your eyes!'

Gran did as she was told and gazed out, onto her garden. She gasped.

'Goodness me! What's all this? How…?' She turned to look at his parents.

'Billy thought this up,' said Mum.

'An idea he got from one of his clubs.' Dad grinned.

'Billy?' Gran squeezed his shoulder. 'A bird table? And just look at that bath…'

'We're doing a project in gardening club on how to attract birds into your garden,' said Billy, voice bubbling with enthusiasm. 'They need all the help they can get, at the moment, what with people tarmacing over their lawns or putting up decking. Miss said the bird population is falling and seeing as, well…' His voice wavered. 'I know you're missing Sky, so I thought you might like to watch wild birds in the garden instead.'

'Oh Billy…' said Gran, cheeks tinged pink, eyes all shiny. 'What a lovely idea. You're a good boy.'

'It'll take a while for them to keep coming regularly,' continued Billy, as a warmth filled his chest. 'And the bushes all need to grow bigger.'

'I love it…' She patted Dad's arm and hugged Mum, before giving Billy's shoulders another huge squeeze. 'It's the best present I've ever had. Look!' she pointed to the dustbin lid where a couple of black speckled birds vigorously bathed and flapped their wings. 'When those starlings have finished, I shall have to top the water up!'

In fact, as the year went on, Gran often had to fill the dustbin lid. The local birds got used to her putting out various tasty scraps and filling the feeder. Just as Dad had said, in the summer and autumn they enjoyed berries from the new plants. Often, when Billy visited, Gran would be busying around, making fat cakes, cleaning out the feeder or consulting her new bird-watching book. The project had also inspired her to take more interest in gardening and she now regularly went into the shed. Eventually, she also found the strength to sort through Gramps' clothes. Billy helped her pack them into bags for the charity shop.

Gran came to love the bird garden as much as she'd loved Sky. Her pride and joy was the nest-box Billy's parents gave her for Christmas. Dad nailed it to the big oak tree. She was so excited the following spring, when a pair of blue tits decided to make it their home. Before long a whole family of them would visit the bird table and take a daily bath. Thanks to her grandson, Gran now had *many* Bluebirds of Happiness to watch.

16

SISTERS, SISTERS

Gwyneth shook her head, marvelling at how gently her granddaughter handled the stick insects. One week ago, ten year old Megan, had finally persuaded her parents to let her buy two. For months the little girl had saved, earning extra pocket money by helping her dad clean the car and doing the washing-up.

'Go, on, Grannie, let Rose climb up you, she's the adventurous one.' Megan held out the spindly little beast, the least striking and smallest of the two.

They were a special breed that grew to the grand length of four inches. Megan placed it on Gwyneth's chest, and the two of them giggled as the insect rocked from side-to-side. The care leaflet said they did this to camouflage themselves in the wild, amongst moving twigs. However, Gwyneth and Megan preferred to believe Rose was something of a disco diva.

'I wonder if they're called stick insects, because they cling on for dear life,' Gwyneth said and finally prised the insect off her beige jumper. She passed it to Megan, who returned it to the tank. 'Are you looking forward to the party tomorrow night, sweetheart?' Gwyneth asked.

'Can't wait! I'm even allowed to stay up right til the end. It's so cool, Grannie, you having your sixty-fifth birthday at the end of term. Mum would never let me go to bed so late if I had school on Monday.' She gave a dimpled smile. 'I've made a special card from that craft kit you bought me. I hope you like it.'

'I'm sure I will, sweetheart.'

With a warm glow in her chest, Gwyneth went downstairs. She plumped up the cushions on the sofa and sat down to continue her cross-stitching. Hopefully her daughter, Karen, would soon be back from work. Gwyneth needed to get back to her own house and begin preparations for tomorrow's big night. She bit her lip. Everyone was in for a great surprise.

Gwyneth put down her needle for a moment and thought ahead to the restaurant meal. What wonderful outfit would her older sister, Sandra, wear? Chalk and cheese they were, that's what people in the village had always said of the two sisters. Teenage Sandra had adored the new fashions from America and spent months begging Mum and Dad to buy a record player. Gwyneth chuckled as she recalled her sister's first ever boyfriend, Tom Parker, the barber's son, with his drainpipe trousers and Teddy Boy hairstyle. Whereas Gwyneth was more of a homebody, never happier than when watching an episode of *Lassie* or baking gingerbread with Mum - both of them in their polka dot aprons, listening to the latest Irving Berlin song on the radio.

Yet Gwyneth loved watching her big sister get ready for a night out, as she glossed her lips and pulled on a dance skirt with net petticoats. Sometimes Gwyneth told herself off for not following the latest trends. Whilst she liked to look smart, she simply had no interest in the latest shoe style or mascara colour. This was going to change; better late than never. Tomorrow night she would reveal her new image. She put down her cross-stitch and her mouth went dry. What if she ended up looking like mutton dressed as lamb?

A loud shriek from upstairs interrupted Gwyneth's thoughts and she rushed up to Megan's bedroom. Her granddaughter's face was pressed up against the glass tank.

'I couldn't find Ivy this morning,' Megan said, cheeks flushed. 'I was busy playing with Rose, but there she is, dangling from that leaf. She's shed her skin.'

Gwyneth bent over and gazed through the maze of upright bramble twigs. Sure enough there hung Ivy, still attached to the remains of her old body, mid-air like an acrobat. All shiny and new, she looked like a real star compared to boring, brown Rose.

'Isn't she beautiful?' cooed Megan. 'Look at the dark and light greens. She's so much bigger, now. I can't wait to show Mum.'

With pursed lips, Gwyneth gazed at her granddaughter's rapt face, her resolve for tomorrow strengthened. She *would* go ahead with her plan. These were modern times – wasn't everyone supposed to look younger? Over the years Sandra had tried to introduce her to the latest fads – psychedelic prints in the Sixties, flares in the Seventies, aerobics and shoulder pads in the Eighties... Her latest invitation had been to have a fish pedicure. Yet Sandra never pushed these ideas and regularly complimented Gwyneth on her natural looks.

'Your sister's right,' Gwyneth's husband, Bill, would say. 'Dead proud I've always been, to have you on my arm.'

But it was her sixty-fifth and she'd just retired from her job as doctor's receptionist. It was time for a change. Bill was scaling down his hours in the decorating business and they'd made exciting plans. First off, they were going to join a rambling club, and take up bowls. It was a fresh start. Gwyneth had discussed it all with June, her hairdresser, who'd finally agreed to dye her hair an up-to-date shade of red. June's niece worked as a beautician and offered to fit super new nails. Gwyneth had even gone on a shopping trip and bought herself a sparkly frock.

The next twenty-four hours flew by and as they got out of the car at the thatched cottage pub, Gwyneth's heart raced. She took Bill's hand and they walked up the path, lined with orange roses. The Cricketers Arms was where she and Bill had celebrated their ruby wedding anniversary, last year, and every December the whole family met there for a Christmas meal.

'I just need to powder my nose, love,' she said to Bill, after waving to the landlord and his wife.

'You look perfect as you are. Happy Birthday, darling,' he whispered, before ducking under the mahogany beamed archway and entering the restaurant.

She glanced ahead of him, just making out their table and the rest of the family – Bill's brother and Dad, young Megan's cousins… Sandra was laughing loudly and stood out in a shimmery, purple top and new blonde highlights. Stomach churning, Gwyneth entered the Ladies and stood in front of the mirror. She re-applied her new make-up and smoothed down some loose strands of hair. With a deep breath she headed for the restaurant, to join everyone.

'Wow, Grannie, you look amazing,' Megan said and ran up to give her a big hug.

'Doesn't she just,' said Bill, grinning. 'I'm the luckiest man in the world.'

'You look lovely, Mum,' said Karen and gave her the

thumbs up.

'Gwynnie! You look fabulous.' Sandra passed her a glass of wine and the two women sat down next to each other, at the table. 'That eyeshadow is gorgeous... but what happened to the red dye?' she whispered.

'I decided it just wasn't me.' Gwyneth said, her heart beating slower now. She smiled and glanced down at her silk cream blouse and tailored trousers. That afternoon, in the hairdresser's, she'd admitted to herself just in time, that she wouldn't feel comfortable in the sparkly frock and quite liked her grey hair. June had let out a sigh of relief – said she couldn't agree more because it showed off her twinkly blue eyes. So, instead the hairdresser had cut some subtle layers into the silver bob and her niece tossed aside the false nails, instead painting Gwyneth's own short but neat ones. Then they'd both helped her choose a suitable eyeshadow and flattering lipgloss. Gwyneth had been thrilled at what a difference a few small changes could make.

'I've always envied your natural hair,' beamed Sandra.

'I just haven't got the courage to colour my hair like yours,' said Gwyneth, at the same time.

'Really?' they both chorused.

Gwyneth squirmed in her seat. 'Well, yes, I mean, you always look so glamorous, although, to be perfectly honest, I'm, um, not sure the bright colours would suit me.'

Sandra cleared her throat. 'Hmm, I mean, I'd love to stop dying my hair, you look great, but I don't think grey would go with my wardrobe...'

The two women looked at each other and chuckled.

'Sounds like we're both comfortable in our own skins,' said Sandra and squeezed her younger sister's hand.

'Look after this for me, Grannie,' whispered Megan, an hour or two later, as everyone finished their chocolate gateau. She held out a box that she'd been furtively showing the other children all evening.

'Is there a stick insect in there, by any chance?' said Gwyneth, with a wink at Sandra. No doubt Megan had smuggled Ivy to the party so that she could show off her new skin.

Sandra took the box and lifted the lid. There were two insects inside.

'I couldn't leave one at home,' whispered Megan. 'Ivy's colouring is brill and Rose's disco moves are so cute. Everyone is well impressed with them both. I'm so glad Mum and Dad let me get two.'

Gwyneth closed the lid, whilst Megan disappeared to drink her coke. Across the table, she caught Sandra's eye. The two sisters smiled.

17

THE ULTIMATE HERO

Jane had always had a weakness for men in uniform. *An officer and a gentleman* was her favourite film. Heroes made her pulse race and over the years she'd dated several guys who fulfilled her fantasies. Except no more. She'd decided the road to happiness didn't require a detour at the police station or a trip on a fire engine.

This was a shame, as Jane had become an expert at polishing boots and sewing buttons back onto neatly starched jackets and shirts. But enough was enough! A fortnight before Christmas, her latest dapper beau had ended their relationship. Apparently he'd been called away on some special mission. Yeah, right. She'd never really believed he worked for the SAS and was best mates with Chris Ryan.

With a sigh, she walked down the icy high street. Just one week to the Christmas Eve party at work and she had no one to accompany her. There was nothing worse than being single during the festive season, with everyone else in happy pairs, eyes all shiny as they looked forward to magic moments under the mistletoe.

Yet the single life could be a good thing, she told herself optimistically. At least that way, she wouldn't get her heart broken and it would give her plenty of time to dedicate to her career. Maybe she'd get a promotion. Yes, Jane decided, that was it – no more men, in uniform or otherwise. This would be her early New Year's resolution, along with giving up chocolate and... and getting a new, dynamic look.

As if on cue, she passed a newly-opened salon, which advertised a special introductory offer. Jane had never been able to resist a bargain.

'Have you any appointments for right this minute?' she asked. 'I need a new style, for Christmas and noticed your offer of half-price colours.'

Two hours later, Jane stood up from the hairdresser's chair, her frizzy brown hair now in a sleek bob, with seasonal red and gold lowlights threaded through. Feeling ten feet tall, she turned sideways in the mirror. What an improvement! After paying, she strode out of the salon and into town, past bustling shoppers and the occasional man working as Father Christmas in some store. One in a baggy jacket and poorly-fitted beard winked and her cheeks tinged pink. So much for that New Year's resolution! Perhaps she'd been too hasty. That man certainly had nice eyes and all her happily married friends proved that there were plenty of decent blokes out there.

Jane continued her walk and kept catching sight of herself in shop windows. Hmm... Cutting out chocolate, that was definitely a good resolution, and perhaps she should abstain from calorific wine, as well. Before her so-called para-trooper boyfriend, she'd dated a comfy, hunky fireman and still had the flabby thighs and a muffin top to remember him by. His mum was a friendly Jamaican woman and had taught Jane how to cook exotic dishes beyond her dreams – and well beyond her daily fat allowance, as well.

Jane took a deep breath and pushed a trolley into the supermarket. Okay, so no men, no chocolate and no wine

– she repeated this mantra as she started to shop. Resolutely, she ignored the flirtatious smile from the store manager and walked straight down the aisles of booze and sweets, like a horse with blinkers on. Finally, Jane stopped by the discount section and sifted through the dented tins and packets of food that were near their sell-by date, on the bottom shelf. As festive music played, she straightened up. That was when an arresting figure, in red and white, caught her eye, from further down the aisle.

Oh god. Nice uniform, compared to some of the other Santas. Admittedly, it wasn't the sexiest of outfits, but at least this one was sleek and smart. What's more, its tightness hinted at a firm body underneath. Must resist, she told herself. Heart racing, Jane swivelled around and headed straight for the till.

Without turning back, she left the building but it was too late. She knew she'd return tomorrow. After a night dreaming of overflowing sacks and jingly sleigh rides, Jane managed to get through a day at work. Then straight after the factory klaxon sounded at five o'clock, she grabbed her coat and hurried into town. Perhaps that lush Father Christmas would no longer be there and she'd find the strength to stick to her New Year Resolutions.

But it was no good, the festive figure was there again, looking more seductive than ever before. Jane gritted her teeth, trying not to imagine how smooth he'd feel, under that festive coat and belt. However, talk about Mission Impossible. Within the hour, they were both back at her flat, on the sofa. Soft music played in the background and she'd double-checked that her mobile phone was switched off.

Okay, so Jane was a quick worker, but where was the harm in that? Needs must and she'd had a miserable few days, working out why her last boyfriend had left. In fact, she told Santa-man all about it, as they sat here and what a hero! It was a long time since a companion had listened to her every word, without yawning or butting in with stories about their action-packed day. Mmm… Attentiveness was such a turn-on.

Yet what about her New Year's resolutions? Aarghh! All of a sudden, Jane felt completely weak-willed. In desperation, she sat on her hands and tried to focus. However, it was no good and, unable to control her urges, Jane took her very own Santa into the bedroom.

As they lay back on the sheets together, she started to remove the jolly outfit, hands shaking as her fingers touched the silken, mocha back. Just look at that physique! Plus most Santas probably reeked of reindeer and pine needles, whereas… Oh my. What a delicious smell. Unable to restrain herself any longer, Jane leaned in close.

'Come here, Santa Baby,' she murmured and seconds later, her bed-fellow's dark mouth melted against her lips. Losing all control, she tore off the rest of the uniform and bit off her Santa's head! Forget uniformed men with all-action jobs - the ultimate hero was ten inches tall and made from chocolate.

18

COCO AND BISCUITS

'Poor Gill,' said Norah, as she stood by the front window, which she did every evening in the summer, right on eight o'clock. Having spent the evening in the lounge, reading or listening to the radio with her husband, she would cast an eye over her favourite shrubs, check for dead heads or random branches that might need pruning. Then it was into the kitchen to fetch tea and biscuits for her and John. Any later would give her indigestion in bed, any earlier and her stomach would gurgle in the night with hunger.

'What's the matter, love?' said John and looked up from his crossword puzzle.

'Gill must have just got back from work. The car door slamming caught my attention. I couldn't help noticing her eyes, all red and swollen.'

John took off his glasses. 'Not good news then, for the rescue centre?'

Norah shrugged. Gill worked all hours in the local cat sanctuary which had run into debt over the last year. What with the recession, people couldn't afford to donate much money or spare tins of cat food.

'I think I'll invite her in for a nice cup of tea, if that's all right with you,' said Norah. 'She might want to talk.'

Gill had never got married or had children, but always said the staff and cats at the centre were her family. And John and Norah always did their bit – she was a regular guest at their house and often joined them for a roast at Easter and over Christmas.

'Good idea, love,' said John. 'Why don't I leave you to it in the lounge? It's been such a warm day - I could do with watering the back garden.'

Fifteen minutes later, the two women sat on the floral sofa, despite Gill's protestations that her trousers were probably covered in cat hair. Norah passed her a digestive.

'So, um, things aren't looking hopeful?' she asked.

Gill ran a hand through her greying bob.

'It's worse than I thought,' she said and took a sip of tea. 'We can't even afford to hold on to all the animals we've got. I was hoping if we at least closed our doors to new cats, that we could somehow manage until things picked up, but...' Gill's voice wavered. 'The kittens are easy to rehome. It looks as if we might have to reduce overall numbers by putting down some of the residents who've been with us for a while.'

Norah put down her plate and squeezed Gill's hand. Having previously owned two tabbies, she was a cat lover herself. Last year the most recent one had died, aged sixteen, just before Norah's seventy-fifth birthday.

'No, we won't get another,' she'd said to Gill, at the time. 'John's tempted but, well, taking on an animal, it's a commitment. Who knows what's around the corner for us health-wise? Anything could happen, like when John strained his back last month. What if we couldn't look after it properly? It wouldn't be fair.'

With an arm around his wife's shoulders, John had said that was typical of responsible Norah. Every present she bought for the grandchildren was checked thoroughly for health and safety issues. She still helped out once a week at the local infants school and served coffee and cake at the church every third Sunday, after the morning service. Doing the right thing was important to her.

'I know we're only a small centre, but it's hard enough finding time to make plans for raising money,' said Gill. 'It's crucial that we form some constructive ideas as soon as possible, but what with manning the phones and cleaning out pens... Everyone seems to be ringing up for kittens at the minute.'

Norah put down her cup. 'Why don't you let me help out tomorrow? I could answer the phone for you, even if I just take messages. And as long as I don't have to bend over too much, I'm sure I could help fill water and food bowls. That way you and the other staff could get together and brainstorm some ideas.'

'Really?' Gill sat more upright. 'I mean, the office is, um, a bit scruffy and it can get draughty... Are you sure?'

'I may be a decade or so older than you, but I'm not made of porcelain,' said Norah, a twinkle in her eye.

For the first time Gill smiled. 'Oh thank you, Norah. I'd really appreciate it. Would you be able to meet me by the car at a quarter to eight tomorrow morning?'

'Of course.' That fitted in perfectly. Norah was an early riser and always ate her breakfast at seven.

Indeed, by lunch time the next day, Norah had settled into the rescue centre and already taken several calls about strays, lost cats and as Gill said, people looking for kittens. She'd also made everyone a coffee, found a duster to clean the desk and done some filing. Plus, she'd made a friend: fifteen year old Coco, a Tortoiseshell with black-chocolate fur and a striking beige stripe down her nose. She was quite the prettiest cat, Norah decided, despite the bitten ear and good left hook she displayed if anyone tried to budge her.

'We let her sit on the desk,' Gill had explained, on their arrival. 'She won't bother you, but might need lifting down when her meal is due. Coco is a creature of habit and will let you know when to feed her.' Gill had chuckled. 'Bang on twelve she'll give her fiery Tortoiseshell meow…'

Norah brushed down her blouse and looked at the clock – it was one minute to midday. This was also her lunch time and right now at home, she would have been preparing sandwiches or soup for her and John. Instead, Norah took out her packed lunch box and was about to prise off the Tupperware lid when, right on cue, there was the loudest of meows.

'Goodness me, Gill was right!' she said to Coco. 'And that sounded just like you said "Now!" How about a please or thank you?' Norah smiled. 'Come on, old girl, let's lift you down to your bowl, for lunch.' The cat raised her stripy nose, eyes narrowing a little, as if to say "less of the old".

It was twelve fifteen before Norah ate her sandwich. She'd waited for Coco to eat and drink and then lifted the puss back up onto the desktop. In fact Norah quite enjoyed the feline company and the background purr. Later in the afternoon, she was even allowed a stroke and tickle of those paws.

'Thanks so much for helping out, Norah,' said Gill, after she finally emerged from the staff meeting. 'Right, let's get going.' She took out her car keys.

'It's been my pleasure.' Norah picked up her handbag. A lump in her throat, she thought about Coco and the other cats she'd met that day – ginger Barney, with his white bib and boots, and ten year old Ebony with her wonky whiskers. How could she let anything happen to them?

'So, what have you decided,' she asked, Gill, 'because I'll do whatever it takes to save each one? Perhaps I could run one of those home garage sales, to raise funds. John often talks about the items we've harboured in the loft, over the years. I'm sure our old crockery sets and ornaments are in good condition and might attract buyers from our estate. I could bake cupcakes and offer them to passers-by for a pound each... We'd hand out your leaflets, to explain the rescue centre's situation and where the proceeds will go. If necessary, I'll knock on every door in the neighbourhood, to find each of these little characters the home they deserve.'

Gill laughed. 'Oh Norah, what a good friend you are, but I hope it won't come to us pacing the streets. We're feeling much more positive and plan to organise a sponsored walk and charity fête. Your garage sale sounds like a good idea. Perhaps we can raise the funds we need, after all.'

'Will you still have to put down some cats?' asked Norah, with a sideways glance at Coco who swiped at a passing fly. For one moment she could just imagine the old puss as a kitten, stalking shadows and chasing her tail.

'I couldn't say definitely,' said Gill, 'but we're feeling much more optimistic.'

Norah reached out and ran her fingers along the tortoiseshell's soft back. 'How about, I mean, I'd have to clear it with John, but as the situation is desperate... The least I can do is adopt Coco.'

'Norah!' Gill's eyes filled. 'That would be wonderful. I've got a spare litter tray somewhere and food to get you started...' Her face broke into a smile and she blew her nose. 'Thank you so much. When could you take her?'

Coco gave a loud meow and both women laughed. Norah shook her head. It really did sound as if the cat said "Now!"

***

Norah stood by the front window, which she did every evening in the summer, right on eight o'clock. Then she went into the kitchen, fetched herself and John two biscuits each and set the plates down in the lounge. Coco sat making eyes at John.

'She's a terrible flirt,' he said, with a lopsided grin, and duly got to his feet and lifted her onto Norah's lap.

The Tortoiseshell settled down, whilst Norah held her plate above the cat's head. She no longer drank her usual tea, for fear the hot drink would spill onto the animal's head. But, Norah decided, sometimes a change was as good as a rest and ending the day with Coco and biscuits, was very pleasant indeed.

19
A CHRISTMAS WISH

Janet turned over in bed and lazily persuaded herself that she hadn't heard a noise. Perhaps, like the other night, she'd left the utility room open and her cat, Smudge, had escaped and was taking a tour of the house. Janet chuckled. He really was a scamp. Perhaps he had unrolled a ball of her best cashmere wool.

With a yawn, she closed her eyes again. It was Christmas Eve. She really had to sleep. Tomorrow would be busy, what with Mum and Dad coming around for the day. Tony, her policeman husband, was out on the beat. Since they'd had the baby, six months earlier, Janet wished that he had a less dangerous, nine til five job. Not that she minded the nights on her own. Janet had always liked the tranquillity of darkness. But Tony was a dad now and shift-work could make family life more difficult.

Once more, she opened her eyes. What *was* that noise? It couldn't be Megan - the only sound their baby daughter made at night was a wail when her dummy dropped out. That meant mischievous Smudge had knocked over something in the lounge. Janet got out of bed and slipped on her dressing gown. So as not to wake Megan, she crept downstairs, on tip-toe. She stood in the hallway for a moment and listened for mews. Strangely, the only sound she heard was jolly humming.

Janet pushed open the lounge door. To her

amazement, light from the street lamp outside revealed an old man. He was bent over, placing a gold-wrapped present under the tree.

'Who are you?' she said, trying to understand why she felt perfectly calm. The man had a white beard and wore a red suit. Next to him on the floor was a big red sack. His shoulders were covered in a black powder. Under any other circumstances her question would have seemed needless. He stood up.

'Goodness, hello Janet, sorry, I didn't mean to startle you, dear.' His eyes crinkled. 'Don't you remember who I am?'

'How do you know my name?' she said, brow furrowed. Perhaps this was a dream.

'Janet Pritchard. I never forget the names of children who were good. Such red curly hair you had! And you always asked for books.' He chuckled. 'They really used to weigh down my sack.'

'I… how… yes, but…' Janet stared at him. It was true. She'd read voraciously as a child and these days straightened her hair. 'It's Janet Jones now,' she stuttered. Father Christmas? Nah. He only existed in children's stories.

'You always slept with Boo-Boo.'

Her mouth fell open. Yet how did he know about her favourite cuddly bear? It had been lost one Christmas, probably thrown away with all the wrappings. Janet would have liked to pass it on to Megan.

'How did you get in?' she asked, ever practical and focussing again.

He brushed the soot off his shoulders. 'Chimneys are a bit of a squeeze these days. I have to use my magic to slide down.' He beamed. 'Go back to bed, dear. Let me leave my present for little Megan, and then I'll be gone.' His deep voice softened. 'Tell me, what would the grown-up Janet like this year?'

Her eyes glanced at a photo of her husband, in uniform.

'I know.' He nodded sagely. 'You'd wish for Tony to have a less dangerous job. Who knows, perhaps your Christmas wish will come true.'

A loud wail pierced the air from upstairs. Janet shook her head. This wasn't real - but just in case it was, she'd better check on Megan.

She stumbled upstairs and sorted out the baby's dummy. Looking at her daughter, she wondered if she'd taken leave of her senses. She should call Tony straightaway, just in case someone had broken in, claiming to be fantastical Santa.

Feeling rather foolish, she rang his number. Ten minutes later, there was a key in the lock. Janet was waiting on the stairs. The front door flew open and Tony came in, accompanied by a female officer.

'Are you all right, darling,' he said and took her hand. 'Where's Megan?'

'Upstairs in bed. We're both fine.' Her cheeks tinged pink. 'I was probably seeing things.'

Sure enough, when they switched on the lights, no one was on the sofa and the back door and windows were still locked. Tony scooted back outside to take a look around.

'Sorry to be a bother, Sharon,' said Janet. 'It must have been a dream.'

'Don't apologise,' said the female officer. 'A burglar dressed as Santa has been doing the rounds all week. It's quite a conundrum. The first two houses he stole from received envelopes of money, the week after the burglary, containing roughly the worth of the goods that had gone missing.' She smiled. 'Reveal information about your past, did he, Janet?' Sharon took out her notebook. 'Has someone called by the house in recent weeks, doing market research for a supposed new chemist opening up in town?'

Janet thought for a moment. 'Yes. About three weeks ago. He was knocking on everyone's doors. Such a nice man, with white hair and…. Ah.'

'Did he ask you lots of questions and offer you free coupons for your time?'

'Yes. He was very friendly. But the man in the lounge tonight… he knew an awful lot about me.'

'Like what?' She patted Janet's arm. 'Don't be embarrassed. He's fooled several people.'

'He knew I liked to read as a child.'

'That's not difficult to work out. Just look at all your full bookcases. You can see into the lounge when the front door's open.'

'He remembered my curly hair.'

The policewoman studied the room and hallway for a moment. 'There – hanging by the coat stand, the montage of family photos… Is that you, as a child, eating ice-cream?'

I smiled. 'Yes. My hair was even curlier back then. But what about Boo-Boo? He remembered my favourite toy.'

At that moment, a shout came from outside and Janet rushed to the window. At the end of the drive, Tony had his hand on the shoulder of a man in a red suit and was calling his colleague. She recognized the culprit, as he passed near the street lamp – it was the market researcher. Janet had forgotten how short he was – nothing like the Santa she'd been talking to, in her lounge.

'Looks like we might have caught him,' said the policewoman and left the house as Tony came back in.

'You okay, love?' said Janet.

Tony nodded. 'It's a bit of a sad case, really. He came quietly – he's a quietly-spoken man; said he'd never meant any harm. His business went bust six months ago and he's struggling to keep paying off his debts. He's living from week to week, juggling his income, and where he can he pays back the people he stole from, slipping an envelope of cash through their door.' Tony shook his head. 'Not that that makes his crime any less serious.'

Janet stared at the Christmas tree.

'What is it, darling?' said her husband.

'That small, gold present...' She bent down and opened up the gift. '*Boo-Boo*?' She bit her lip and stood up, holding the tatty bear.

Tony wrapped his arms round her. 'I should have been here.'

'Nonsense,' she said. 'You know I'm always sensible about checking the doors and windows, last thing at night. Good common sense goes a long way.'

'Still, this confirms that I've made the right decision about work, especially as Megan is often awake during the night. I was going to tell you tomorrow, as a Christmas surprise. I've been offered a desk job, with prospects. I'll be able to help out much more now, with the baby.'

Janet's eyes shone. 'Really? But...Are you sure it'll be enough of a challenge? I wouldn't want you to give up your dreams.'

Tony grinned. 'Dreams change and so do challenges – like learning how to change Megan's nappy as quickly as you! The pay's good, as well. I'd be mad to miss this opportunity. In fact, this job offer came out of the blue, just like magic.'

Janet hugged him tight and could have sworn she heard the distant jingle of sleigh bells. Her chest glowed. Perhaps Santa did grant wishes to grown-ups, as well.

20
A LOST CAUSE

'It's such a cliché.' Juliet groaned. 'Everyone told me it would happen. I insisted it wouldn't.'

'What?' asked her sister, Susan, who had called in after spending the morning on the phone to tradesmen. Her washing machine had leaked the previous evening and her laminate floor was ruined.

'Getting broody – now that Emily is in reception year.' Juliet placed two coffees on the kitchen table. She offered Susan a biscuit and sat down opposite her. 'Other mums warned me that's how I'd feel, when my youngest started school full-time.'

'Have you told Tim?'

The two sisters chuckled. Juliet could just imagine his expression - although it really wasn't a laughing matter. It was hard enough providing two children with everything they required, thanks to the recession.

'No. I'm not deadly serious,' said Juliet. 'Apart from anything else, I've just upped my hours, working freelance.' She gazed out of the window, at the golds and russets of autumn leaves, all the more appealing in October sunlight. 'It's a big change – only having myself to look after during the day now, with just one lunch to make. My only conversation is with online secretarial clients.'

Susan cleared her throat and brushed crumbs off her jumper. 'Perhaps I have a solution that could be mutually beneficial.'

Juliet raised her eyebrows.

'The house is a bit of a mess, thanks to the flooding,' said Susan. 'What with a new floor being laid, the week ahead is going to be noisy. It would only be for a couple of days and…'

Juliet shook her head. 'No way. Come on, Sis – it wouldn't work.'

'You don't know what I'm going to ask!'

'Let me guess. It's to do with your latest feline guests.'

For years, Susan had fostered kittens from the local cat sanctuary, offering them and their mothers a home, whilst they were too small to live in a pen at the rescue centre.

'He's no trouble at all, Jules,' said Susan. 'I would ask another foster lady I know, but she's just taken in a whole litter.'

'I thought you'd given up trying to convert me to being an animal lover, a long time ago?'

'Never,' said Susan. 'It still saddens me to think what you missed out on, as a child.'

Juliet sipped her coffee. 'Your hamster flicked sawdust everywhere and the guinea-pig hutch smelt. I was more than happy just playing with my dolls.'

Susan's eyes twinkled. 'Mum and dad always mused about how different we were - me never happier than when my hands were mucking out hay or gardening; you impossibly neat for a teenager, clothes and hair pristine, room tidier than a shop display window.'

'The last time you asked me to take in a cat was, ooh, years ago, just before Charlotte was born. Tim and I still lived in that flat on Acacia Avenue.' Juliet sighed. 'We had that gorgeous cream leather sofa and the immaculate beech and silver kitchen. There was no way I wanted scratch marks on my furniture or litter-training accidents ruining my plush carpets.'

'This little chap's called Alaska,' said Susan. 'His mum died from an infection last week, just as he turned three months old. They were found in a factory, soon after he was born. Despite everything, though, his purr is the loudest I've ever heard. Yet I suspect he'll spend his whole life in the sanctuary, once he's old enough. Alaska's a bit of a lost cause.

'Why?' Juliet smoothed down her blouse.

'He's white, for a start. People prefer more unusual cats with ginger, tortoiseshell or tabby fur. Plus part of his left ear is missing and his tail is crooked. No one knows why.'

'Well, good luck with placing him,' said Juliet. 'Now, let's get back to your domestic crisis. Do you want to use my washing machine until yours is mended?'

'Pleeaase, Jules. Your conservatory would be perfect for him.'

'Sorry, Susan. It's out of the question. I've no experience of looking after cats. It's probably for the best.'

'But the girls would love to have him stay – especially as they've never had pets of their own.'

'That's emotional blackmail! Anyway, I bought them stick insects.'

Susan raised one eyebrow.

Juliet sighed. 'All right. I can't believe I'm saying this, but he can stay, as long as it's just for a few days.'

'Thanks, Sis, you're the best!' Susan squeezed Juliet's hand. 'I really appreciate your help. And if it doesn't work out, I'll take him straight back and try to make other arrangements.'

'How did I let this happen,' muttered Juliet, a few

hours later, as she sat in the conservatory, staring at the small white kitten. Ocean-blue eyes stared back. Doubtless scared her sister would change her mind, Susan hadn't wasted any time. She'd dropped the kitten off, after lunch, with his litter tray, scratch pad, bed and food. Juliet poured some biscuits into a bowl and sat back in a wicker chair. At least the animal ate tidily and cleaned its face afterwards.

'Right, I'll let you settle in,' she mumbled and shut the conservatory door behind her as she left. When she walked past, ten minutes later, sad blue eyes peered through the glass at her. It brought back memories of Emily and Charlotte's faces when she used to drop them off at nursery for the first few times, years ago.

With a sigh, Juliet went back into the conservatory and sat down. Sun rays streamed onto the floor. Alaska gave a small mew and jumped onto her lap. Susan was right – he had an amazingly loud purr.

'You… But… I've got work to do,' said Juliet, as he lay down and curled into a ball.

Oh dear. Now she'd get nothing done, until it was time to pick Emily and Charlotte up from school. Juliet ran her hand over the small furry back, surprised at how soft it felt. Her fingers stroked the half-bitten ear and Alaska stretched out.

'Mummy! He's so cute!' said Emily, when they all got in at half-past three. Juliet took off her coat and followed her daughters into the conservatory.

'Be careful not to frighten him' said Juliet and passed Charlotte one of the toys Susan had also left – a rod, with a feather on the end. Then she watched the children and Alaska play - or 'Al' as Emily called him.

'Look how high he can jump,' said Charlotte and

giggled as he tried to reach the feather dangling in the air.

A bird flew down onto the lawn outside, and all of a sudden Al went up to the window, crouched down and rocked his back legs. Clouds gathered and before long rain hit the conservatory windows. Fascinated, the kitten swiped at each drop. Everyone laughed.

'Right girls,' said Juliet, 'go and wash your hands before tea. I'll just give Al some more biscuits.' She turned around to find the kitten standing beside a puddle. 'Oh dear. Couldn't you reach the litter tray in time?' It reminded her of the girls when potty training. No harm done. These things happened.

Indeed, it happened again the next morning but Juliet already had a supply of kitchen roll and anti-bacterial spray to hand. He also dug his claws into the wicker chair's cushion. Juliet put him next to the scratch post and gently moved his paws up and down against it, so that he'd know for next time. It reminded her of the time Charlotte crayoned on her bedroom wall paper and afterwards Juliet always made sure her eldest daughter was never far from a big drawing pad.

The next morning, unable to leave Al alone, forlorn face pressed against the glass, Juliet took her lap-top into the conservatory and listened to him trill every time a bird hopped past, outside. She topped up his food bowl and they ate lunch together. Then he napped on her lap. This became their routine for the next couple of days, until one afternoon, later in the week, Susan turned up with a cat carrier.

'Thanks so much, Jules,' said Susan. 'The house is back in one piece. I can take him off your hands.'

'The, um, children will really miss him,' she said. 'Could you wait until Emily and Charlotte come back from school, so that they can say goodbye?'

'Of course.'

'Tim will be sorry to see him go,' Juliet half-smiled. 'I think he's quite liked having another male in the house.'

Susan glanced sideways at her. 'Are you sure he'll be the only one to miss him?'

Juliet's cheeks tinged pink. 'It wasn't as much work as I thought. Since becoming a mum, I guess I worry less about the little things; I'm not as house-proud.'

'Wonders will never cease!'

Affectionately, Juliet clapped her sister on the shoulder.

'Well, you don't need to worry about him,' said Susan. 'Against all the odds, I think I've found him a home.'

Juliet's stomach twisted.

'It's not ideal,' she continued, 'but it's his best chance. A retired lady who lives in a block of flats has agreed to take him on a temporary basis, to see how it goes. Of course, he'll never go outdoors…'

'But Al is itching to get outside!' said Juliet. 'He can't wait to walk in the rain and chase birds.'

'At least he won't spend his life in a pen at the sanctuary.'

'But someone else could offer him so much more.'

Susan nodded. 'Perhaps. But what if this turned out to be his one and only offer of a home? I'm ringing the lady back this evening, to confirm.'

'No, don't! I mean…'

'Jules?'

Juliet cleared her throat. 'Why doesn't he stay here?'

Susan's jaw dropped open. 'You're really prepared to make a long-term commitment?'

With a smile, Juliet shrugged. 'Like I said, after all

these years changing nappies and cleaning up sick, a kitten's no bother at all.'

Juliet was still smiling later that evening. With the children in bed, Al slept on her lap, once more. She ran her hand along his crooked tail and glowed warm inside, as he purred. Who was a lost cause now?

21

ONE LUMP OR TWO?

Wendy took a deep breath and pulled off her apron. It wasn't every day your new boss came to dinner and things weren't running as smoothly as she had hoped. The steak and kidney pie pastry was too crumbly and she couldn't find her favourite lipstick. John had made an effort, and even bought two candleholders to match their tablecloth. Yet as seven o'clock approached, he'd tugged continuously at the collar of his new shirt and tutted about the expensive bottle of red she'd bought.

'What's wrong with our usual plonk?' he asked for the tenth time, just as the doorbell rang.

'Mr Hamilton… Ron… knows a lot about wine,' she said and they headed to the front door. 'I want to make a good impression. You know the rumour, John – that he's been brought in to rationalize the company. At my age, I'll never find another job this good.'

'And why the sudden menu change?'

She checked her hair in the hallway mirror and wished that she'd got her grey roots done. 'Because I heard him say in the office yesterday, that steak and kidney pie was his favourite.'

'But after all the practice you put in?' He gave a wry smile.

Poor John – she'd made him eat salmon with hollandaise sauce three nights in a row. There was a jug of leftover sauce in the fridge as she'd accidentally made too much. The last batch had been lumpy, but she hadn't liked to throw it out - not with the recession and threat of unemployment.

'You look fine, love,' he said.

She nodded. The doorbell rang again and quickly she opened the door.

'Hello, Mr Hamilton,' she stuttered.

'Now, now, Wendy, I've told you before, call me Ron.' A chubby face came forward and he kissed her on either cheek. Nervously she smiled and stepped back to admire his navy gold-buttoned blazer and pristine slacks. He blustered in, looking every bit as smart as he did at the office.

Ron eyed her up and down. 'Charming as usual, Wendy!' he boomed and then turned to his wife. 'This is Ann.'

Wendy smiled at the petite lady by his side who wore a simple black dress with a purple shawl. The outfit perfectly complimented her glamorous ash-blonde bob. Suddenly Wendy felt as plain as the hallway's beige carpet, in her trousers and blouse.

John stepped forward in his best jumper and cords and shook Ron's hand. 'I'm John. Great to meet you at last,' he said. 'Come and sit down. Can I get you both a drink?'

Slowly Wendy's stomach unknotted as her husband handed around nibbles and dutifully asked the couple about their recent move to the area. Whilst the pie cooked, she joined them in the lounge. She laughed at Ron's jokes and listened intently to his plans for the department. On and off she heard John and Ann discussing the weather and the local garden centre - whereas Ron talked of the phenomenon of internet billionaires and team-building trips to the Swiss Alps.

Ron was a jet-setter, a man with big ideas. This last month in the office had been exciting, with his stories of working abroad and tales of the huge contracts he'd landed. Strangely Debs, his secretary, wasn't that fond of him and occasionally rolled her eyes behind his back.

'Let me help you dish up,' beamed John as Wendy stood up and ushered the guests to the table.

'What are you doing?' she whispered, once they were alone in the kitchen. 'You're the host. Go and fill up their glasses and make conversation.'

'I needed a break.' He exhaled. 'That Ron… Does he have to speak so loud? And is there *any* subject he doesn't know about? As for that compass-sized watch and the way he replied to a text whilst you were talking…'

'That was business,' muttered Wendy.

John shook his head and grabbed the fancy bottle of red, before leaving the kitchen. Ten minutes later they were all tucking into the pie with steamed vegetables and mash.

'Pass me the salt, Wendy,' said Ron. She winced as he shook it vigorously over the potatoes and hoped the pie was seasoned enough.

'This is delicious,' said Ann and glared at her husband. 'You must give me the recipe.'

'I always find steak and kidney pie goes well with roasted Mediterranean vegetables,' remarked Ron and pushed his peas to the side of the plate.

'Um, yes, I'm sure you're right,' said Wendy and wished she and John had travelled more. To her horror, her husband lifted a bottle of their usual cheap plonk off the floor and filled his own glass.

'What were you thinking?' she said when everyone

had finished the main course and he brought the dirty plates into the kitchen.

'I don't like that rich wine,' he said. 'It'll give me a headache. Talking of which, I'll quickly make myself some custard to have with the pud. I don't want to risk eating chocolate, you know it doesn't agree with me.'

'But it's only a white chocolate sauce!'

'Sorry, love,' said John. 'I can't risk one of my migraines.'

Wendy tutted. 'I'll make it. You'll take twice as long.' Normally she didn't mind his little foibles, but why did John have to be such a fuss-bucket, tonight of all nights? A scratching at the door distracted her and she let in the cat. You'll eat anything, won't you my lovely, she cooed to the tabby, still annoyed with her husband when she eventually carried in the raspberry sponge.

After several mouthfuls, Ron put down his spoon. 'Not bad,' he said. 'I had a dessert like this in Paris, once – they served it with a fantastic berry coulis.'

'You can't go wrong with chocolate, though,' smiled Ann. 'John's lucky to be married to such a good cook.'

John had been quiet for a while. 'I am, indeed,' he finally said, after he'd swallowed the last mouthful. 'Now you put your feet up, love,' he said to his wife, 'whilst I make coffee.'

He took longer than Wendy expected but eventually appeared with a tray and four full cups. He'd even remembered to put out a bowl of the posh sugar cubes she'd bought.

'One lump or two, Ron?' she asked.

'Sweeteners, please, Wendy, if you've got them.' He patted his belly. 'The wife doesn't let me have pure sugar.'

'I'm sure this once won't matter,' said Ann, an

apologetic look on her face.

John sat down with his cup of tea. 'Caffeine keeps me awake,' he explained to their guests. 'I never drink coffee after six pm.'

'Do my job for one day and you'll sleep like a baby, no matter what,' said Ron. 'Wendy's one of my best workers. I bet she's flat out as soon as her head hits the pillow, like me.'

A glazed smile fixed onto John's face. His brow didn't relax until the guests waved goodbye and drove off in their car.

'That went okay, don't you think?' he said and drew the curtains. 'It doesn't sound as if Ron will be laying you off. He's a bit of a nit-picker though. I felt sorry for Ann. Some of his comments were just plain rude.'

'*He's* a nit-picker?' Wendy couldn't help grinning. 'What about you with your cup of tea and cheap plonk? And at least he's trying to watch his weight.'

John snorted and sat down on the sofa. 'Swapping sweeteners for sugar won't make much difference if he drinks that much.'

She shrugged and went into the kitchen but yes, even she'd been surprised at how much her boss had complained. That was one thing she admired about John – he always put other people's feelings first. He may have been set in his ways, but would never make a fuss in someone else's house. In fact, the last time they'd eaten at her sister's, he'd not said a word when she served chocolate mousse.

Whereas, thinking about it, Ron had made the new intern cry, pulling to bits the document she'd spent days working on. Plus he'd insulted a colleague's new hairdo and complained loudly when their lovely cleaner forgot to empty his bin. As for his secretary, Wendy now remembered a comment he'd once made about her coffees never tasting right.

Deciding that perhaps her boss wasn't as perfect as she once thought, she stacked the plates and pudding bowls, with John's on top. After the washing-up, she'd make him a nice mug of tea. She reached to turn on the taps, but something caught her eye in her husband's empty dish.

Yellow lumps? Her cheeks flushed hot as she lifted the bowl to her nose. Poor John. And he hadn't said a word. Wendy carried the empty bowl into the lounge and raised her eyebrows.

'Ah…' He cleared his throat.

'Why didn't you say anything?' she said. 'The cat distracted me and I forgot all about making the custard. I must have just grabbed the jug of Hollandaise sauce out of the fridge. My mind was elsewhere.'

'I know how important tonight was to you, love. I didn't want to make a fuss. Sorry I took a while to make the coffees.' He grinned. 'I thought I was going to be sick.'

Eyes tingling, she went over to the armchair and kissed the top of his head. John slipped his arm around her waist and pulled her onto his lap.

'Thank heavens there wasn't any spare gravy around,' he said and his eyes twinkled. 'Otherwise who knows what might have ended up on his Lordship's raspberry sponge. A mistake like that could have cost you your job!'

ABOUT THE AUTHOR

Samantha lives in Cheshire with her lovely family, and two cats who think they are dogs. She writes stories for mainstream women's magazines and her work appears regularly in The People's Friend. Her passion for short fiction evolved from several years of writing novels. Currently, her agent is submitting "Doubting Abbey", her latest romantic comedy.

More information about Samantha can be found at: http://samanthatonge.co.uk/

Alfie Dog Fiction

Taking your imagination for a walk

For hundreds of short stories, collections
and novels visit our website at
www.alfiedog.com

Join us on Facebook
http://www.facebook.com/AlfieDogLimited

Printed in Great Britain
by Amazon.co.uk, Ltd.,
Marston Gate.